"You don't have . . ." Rosella stopped.

Something funny was happening in her mouth. Had she lost a tooth? There was something hard under her tongue. And something hard in her cheek. "Excuse me." Now there was something in her other cheek. She spat delicately into her hand.

They weren't teeth. She was holding a diamond and two opals.

"There, dearie." Ethelinda smiled. "Isn't that nice?"

BOOKS BY
Gail Carson Levine

Ella Enchanted
Dave at Night
The Wish
The Two Princesses of Bamarre

THE PRINCESS TALES:
The Fairy's Mistake
The Princess Test
Princess Sonora and the Long Sleep
Cinderellis and the Glass Hill
For Biddle's Sake
The Fairy's Return

The Princess Tales

Volume One

The Fairy's Mistake • The Princess Test
Princess Sonora and the Long Sleep

Gail Carson Levine

ILLUSTRATED BY
Mark Elliott

HarperTrophy®
An Imprint of HarperCollinsPublishers

Harper Trophy® is a registered trademark of HarperCollins Publishers Inc.

The Princess Tales, Volume I

The Fairy's Mistake
Text copyright © 1999 by Gail Carson Levine
Illustrations copyright © 1999 by Mark Elliott

The Princess Test
Text copyright © 1999 by Gail Carson Levine
Illustrations copyright © 1999 by Mark Elliott

Princess Sonora and the Long Sleep
Text copyright © 1999 by Gail Carson Levine
Illustrations copyright © 1999 by Mark Elliott

Library of Congress Cataloging-in-Publication Data
Levine, Gail Carson.
    The princess tales : volume I / Gail Garson Levine ; illustrated by Mark Elliott.—1st
Harper Trophy ed.
        p.   cm.
    Summary: Humorous retellings of three classic fairy tales, Diamonds and toads, the
Princess and the pea, and Sleeping Beauty, in one volume.
    Contents: The fairy's mistake — The princess test — Princess Sonora and the long sleep.
    ISBN 0-06-051841-3
    [1. Fairy tales. 2. Folklore.] I. Elliott, Mark, ill. II. Title.
PZ8.L4793 Pqe 2003   2002068548
398.82—dc21   CIP
                                                                        AC

Typography by Andrea Vandergrift
❖
First Harper Trophy edition, 2003

Visit us on the World Wide Web!
www.harperchildrens.com

CONTENTS

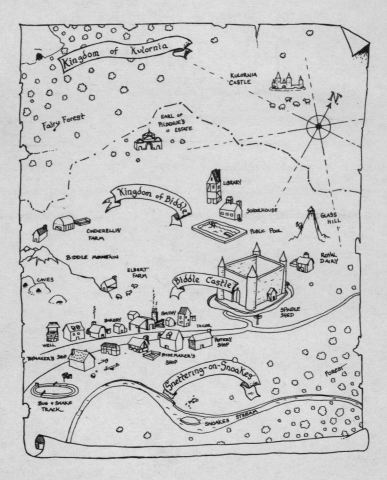

The
Fairy's Mistake

All my thanks
to my wonderful editor, Alix Reid.
Without you, *The Princess Tales*
would never have been told.

—G.C.L.

One

Once upon a time, in the village of Snettering-on-Snoakes in the kingdom of Biddle, Rosella fetched water from the well for the four thousand and eighty-eighth time.

Rosella always fetched the water because her identical twin sister, Myrtle, always refused to go. And their mother, the widow Pickering, never made Myrtle do anything. Instead, she made Rosella do everything.

At the well the fairy Ethelinda was having a drink. When she saw Rosella coming, she changed herself into an old lady. Then she made herself look thirsty.

"Would you like a drink, Grandmother?" Rosella said.

"That would be lovely, dearie."

"SHE SPAT DELICATELY INTO HER HAND."

Rosella lowered her wooden bucket into the well. When she lifted it out, she held the dipper so the old lady could drink.

Ethelinda slurped the water. "Thank you. Your kindness merits a reward. From now—"

"You don't have . . ." Rosella stopped. Something funny was happening in her mouth. Had she lost a tooth? There was something hard under her tongue. And something hard in her cheek. "Excuse me." Now there was something in her other cheek. She spat delicately into her hand.

They weren't teeth. She was holding a diamond and two opals.

"There, dearie." Ethelinda smiled. "Isn't that nice?"

Two

"What took you so long?" Myrtle said when Rosella got home.

"Your sister almost perished from thirst, you lazy-bones," their mother said.

"I gave a drink to . . ." Something was in Rosella's mouth again. It was between her lip and her front teeth this time. "I gave a drink to an old lady." An emerald and another diamond fell out of her mouth. They landed on the dirt floor of the cottage.

"It was more important— What's that?" Myrtle said.

"What's that?" the widow said.

They both dove for the jewels, but Myrtle got there first.

"Rosella darling," the widow said, "sit down. Make

yourself comfortable. Now tell us all about it. Don't leave anything out."

There wasn't much to tell, only enough to cover the bottom of Myrtle's teacup with gems.

"Which way did the old lady go?" Myrtle asked.

Rosella was puzzled. "She didn't go anywhere." An amethyst dropped into the teacup.

Myrtle grabbed the bucket and ran.

When she saw Myrtle in the distance, Ethelinda thought Rosella had come back. Only this time she wasn't tripping lightly down the path, smelling the flowers and humming a tune. She was hurtling along, head down, arms swinging, bucket flying. And then Ethelinda's fairy powers told her that this was Rosella's twin sister. Ethelinda got ready by turning herself into a knight.

"Where did the old lady go?" Myrtle said when she reached the well.

"I haven't seen anyone. I've been alone, hoping some kind maiden would come by and give me a drink. I can't do it myself with all this armor."

"What's in it for me if I do?"

The fairy tilted her head. Her armor clanked. "The

happiness of helping someone in need."

"Well, in that case, get your page to do it." Myrtle stomped off.

Ethelinda turned herself back into a fairy. "Your rudeness merits a punishment," she said. But Myrtle was too far away to hear.

Myrtle went through the whole village of Snettering-on-Snoakes, searching for the old lady. The villagers knew she was Myrtle and not Rosella by her scowl and by the way she acted. Myrtle marched into shops and right into people's houses. She opened doors to rooms and even closets. Whenever anyone yelled at her, her only answer was to slam the door on her way out.

While Myrtle was in the village, Rosella went out to her garden to pick peas for dinner. As she worked, she sang.

Oh, May is the lovely month.
Sing hey nonny May-o!
Oh, June is the flower month.
Sing hey nonny June-o!
Oh, July is the hot month.
Sing hey nonny July-o!

And so on. While she sang, gems dropped from her mouth. It still felt funny, but she was getting used to it. Except once she popped a pea into her mouth as she sang, and she almost broke a tooth on a ruby.

Rosella had a sweet voice, but Prince Harold, who happened to be riding by, wasn't musical. He wouldn't have stopped, except he spotted the sapphire trembling on Rosella's lip. He watched it tumble into the vegetables.

He tied his horse up at the widow Pickering's picket fence.

Rosella didn't see him, and she went on singing.

Oh, November is the harvest month.
Sing hey nonny November-o!
Oh, December is the last month.
Sing hey . . .

Prince Harold went into the garden. "Maiden . . ."

Rosella looked up from her peas. A man! A nobleman! She blushed prettily.

She wasn't bad-looking, Prince Harold thought. "Pardon me," he said. "You've dropped some jewels. Allow me."

"Oh! Don't trouble yourself, Sir." Another sapphire and a moonstone fell out of Rosella's mouth.

Harold had a terrible thought. Maybe they were just glass. He picked up a stone. "May I examine this?"

Rosella nodded.

It didn't look like glass. It looked like a perfect diamond, five carats at least. But if the gems were real, why was she leaving them on the ground? He held up a jewel. "Maiden, is this really a diamond?"

"I don't know, Sir. It might be."

A topaz hit Prince Harold in the forehead. He caught it as it bounced off his chin. "Maiden, have jewels always come out of your mouth?"

Rosella laughed, a lovely tinkling sound. "Oh no, Sir. It only began this afternoon when an old lady— I think she may have been a fairy—"

They *were* real then! Harold knelt before her. "Maiden, I am Prince Harold. I love you madly. Will you marry me?"

Three

Rosella didn't love the prince madly, but she liked him. He was so polite. And she thought it might be pleasanter to be a princess than to be the widow Pickering's daughter and Myrtle's sister. Besides, it could be against the law to say no to a prince. So she said yes, and dropped a garnet into his hand.

"I'm sorry, sweetheart. I didn't hear you."

"Yes, Your Highness."

Clink. Clink. Two more garnets joined Harold's collection. "You must say, 'Yes, Harold,' now that we're betrothed."

"Yes, Harold."

Clink.

The fairy Ethelinda was delighted that Rosella was going to be a princess. She deserves it, the fairy thought. Ethelinda was pleased with herself for having given Rosella the perfect reward.

The widow Pickering agreed to the marriage. But she insisted that Harold give her all the gems Rosella had produced before their engagement. The widow was careful not to mention Myrtle. She didn't want the prince to know that Rosella had a twin sister who would also have a jewel mine in her mouth. After all, what if he took Myrtle away too?

Prince Harold swung Rosella up on his horse. He asked her to hold an open saddlebag on her lap. Then he mounted in front of her. As they rode off, he asked her about her garden, about the weather, about fly fishing, about anything.

The widow stood at the fence and waved her handkerchief. As she turned to go back into the cottage, she saw her favorite daughter in the distance. Myrtle was loping along, swinging the bucket. The widow opened the gate and followed her daughter into the house. "Darling, speak to me."

Myrtle sank into their only comfortable chair. "Hi, Mom. The stupid old lady wasn't—" There was a tickle in the back of her throat. What was going on?

"HE ASKED HER ABOUT HER GARDEN, ABOUT THE WEATHER . . . ABOUT ANYTHING."

It felt like her tongue had gotten loose and was flopping around in her mouth. Could she be making jewels too? Did it happen just by going to the well? Whatever it was—diamond or pearl or emerald—it wanted to get out. Myrtle opened her mouth.

A garter snake slithered out.

The widow screamed and jumped onto their other chair. "Eeeeek! Get that thing out of here! Myrtle!" She pointed a shaking finger. "There it is! Get it! Eeeeek!"

Myrtle didn't budge. She stared at the snake coiling itself around a bedpost. How had this happened if the old lady wasn't at the well? The knight? The knight! The old lady had turned herself into a knight.

Myrtle jumped up and raced out, taking the bucket with her. "'Bye, Mom," she called over her shoulder. "See you later." Two mosquitoes and a dragonfly flew out of her mouth.

The fairy Ethelinda watched Myrtle scurry down the road. She patted herself on the back for having given Myrtle the perfect punishment.

Four

Prince Harold and Rosella reached the courtyard in front of the prince's palace. He lifted Rosella down from the horse.

"I'm too madly in love to wait," he said. "Let's announce our engagement first thing tomorrow morning, dear heart."

"All right," Rosella said.

Harold only got a measly seed pearl. "Princesses speak in complete sentences, darling."

Rosella took a deep breath for courage. "I'm tired, Your High—I mean Harold. May I rest for a day first?"

But Harold didn't listen. He was too interested in the green diamond in his hand. "I've never seen one of these before, honey bun. We can have the betrothal ceremony at nine o'clock sharp. Your Royal Ladies-in-Waiting will find you something to wear."

Harold snapped his fingers, and a Royal Lady-in-Waiting led Rosella away. They were on the castle doorstep when Harold ran after them.

"Angel, I almost forgot. What would you like served at our betrothal feast?"

Nobody had ever asked Rosella this kind of question before. She'd always had to eat scraps from her mother's and her sister's plates. Nobody had ever asked her what she liked to eat. Nobody had ever asked her opinion about anything.

She smiled happily. "Your—I mean, Harold . . . uh . . . dear, I'd like poached quail eggs and roasted chestnuts for our betrothal feast." Six identical emeralds the color of maple leaves in May dropped from Rosella's mouth.

The Royal Lady-in-Waiting, who was at Rosella's elbow, gasped.

"Look at these!" Harold said. "They're gorgeous. So you want wild boar for dinner?" He didn't give Rosella time to say she hated wild boar. "What do you know? It's my favorite too. I'll go tell the cook." He rushed off.

Rosella sighed.

The fairy Ethelinda, who was keeping an eye on things, sighed too.

⚓ ⚓ ⚓

Myrtle returned to the well, determined to give a drink to anybody who was there. But nobody was. She lowered the bucket into the well anyway.

Nobody showed up.

She had an idea. It was worth a try. She watered the plants that grew around the well. "Dear plants," she began. "You look thirsty. Perhaps a little water would please you. It's no trouble. I don't mind, dear sweet plants."

Whatever was in her mouth was too big to be a jewel, unless it was the biggest one in the world. And a jewel wouldn't feel slimy on her tongue. She opened her mouth. A water bug crawled out. She closed her mouth, but there was more. More slime. She opened her mouth again. Two more water bugs padded out, followed by a black snake.

Giving the plants a drink hadn't done any good. Myrtle dumped the rest of the water on a rose bush. "Drown, you stupid plant," she muttered. A grasshopper landed on a rose.

Myrtle filled her bucket one more time. Then—without saying a single word—she scoured the village again for the rotten fairy who'd done this to her. She swore to herself that she'd pour water down the throat of any stranger she found.

But there were no strangers, so Myrtle threw the bucket into the well and headed for home.

The widow was in the garden. She had dug up the peas and the radishes and the tomato plants. Now she was pawing through the roots, hoping to find some jewels that Prince Harold had missed. When she heard the gate slam shut, she stood up. "Don't say a word if you didn't find that old lady."

Myrtle closed her mouth with a snap. She picked up a stick and scratched in the dirt, "Where's Rosella?"

"She rode off to marry a prince. And like a fool, I let her go, because I thought I had you. You bungler, you idiot, you . . ."

That made Myrtle furious. How could she have known the fairy would turn herself into a knight in so much armor you couldn't even see her—his—face? And hadn't she searched the village twice?

And hadn't she watered those useless plants? Myrtle opened her mouth to give her mother what-for.

But the widow held up her hands and jumped back three feet. "Hush! Shh! Hush, my love. Perhaps I was hasty. We've both had a bad . . ."

Her mother's pleas gave Myrtle a new idea. She picked up the stick again and wrote, "Things are looking up, Mom. It will all be better tomorrow." She dropped the stick and started whistling—and wondering if whistling made snakes and insects too.

It didn't. Too bad, she thought.

Five

Rosella was used to sleeping on the floor, because Myrtle and the widow had always taken the bed. In the palace she got her own bed. It had a canopy and three mattresses piled on top of each other and satin sheets and ermine blankets and pillows filled with swans' feathers.

So she should have gotten a fine night's sleep—except that three Royal Guards stood at attention around her bed all night. One stood at each side of the bed, and one stood at the foot. If she talked in her sleep, they were supposed to catch the jewels and keep them safe for Prince Harold.

Rosella didn't talk in her sleep because she couldn't sleep with people watching her. By morning her throat felt scratchy. She thought she might be coming down with a cold.

Her twelve Royal Ladies-in-Waiting brought breakfast to her at seven o'clock. Scrambled eggs and wild-boar sausages. They shared the sausages while she ate the eggs. Rosella said "please" six times and "thank you" eight times. Each Royal Lady-in-Waiting got one jewel, and they fought over the remaining two.

"Nobody deserves that but me!" yelled one Royal Lady-in-Waiting.

"I work harder than any of you!" yelled another.

"I'm worth ten of each of you, so I should get everything!" shouted a third.

"You have some nerve, thinking . . ."

Rosella put her hands over her ears. She wished she could have ten minutes to herself.

Prince Harold came in. He coughed to get the attention of the Royal Ladies-in-Waiting. Nobody noticed except Rosella, who smiled at him. He'd be handsome, she thought, if he weren't so greedy.

The Royal Ladies-in-Waiting went on arguing.

"How dare you—"

"What do you mean—"

"The first person who—"

"SHUT UP!" Harold roared.

They did.

"You mustn't upset my bride." He went to Rosella, who was eating her breakfast in bed. He put his arm around her shoulder. "Are you all right, sugar plum?"

Rosella nodded. She liked the pet names he called her. But she hoped he wouldn't make her say anything.

"Tell me so I'm sure, lovey-dove."

The fairy Ethelinda was worried.

⚓ ⚓ ⚓

Myrtle, on the other hand, had a great night's sleep. When she woke up, she put paper, a quill pen, and a bottle of ink in a pouch. Then she set out for the village. She'd have a fine breakfast when she got there, and she wouldn't pay a penny for it. As for the bucket she'd thrown down the well, why, she'd have her choice of buckets.

Her first stop was the baker's shop. She's scowling, the baker thought, so it's Myrtle. He scowled right back.

"HE SCOWLED RIGHT BACK."

"Give me three of your freshest muffins," Myrtle said.

She has some nerve, the baker thought. Bossing me— What was coming out of her mouth? Ants! He grabbed his broom and swept them out of his store. He tried to sweep Myrtle out too.

"Cut that out!" Myrtle said. A horsefly flew out of her mouth. A bedbug climbed over the edge of her lip and started down her chin.

The baker swatted the fly. He kept an eye on the bedbug, so he could kill it as soon as it touched the floor.

Myrtle took the pen and paper out of her pouch. "Give me the muffins and I won't say another word," she wrote. "I also want a fourteen-layer cake. It's for my party tomorrow, to celebrate my fourteen-year-and-six-weeks birthday. You're invited. Bring the whole family."

The baker swallowed hard and nodded. "I'll come. We'll all come. We'll be, uh, overjoyed to come." He wrapped up his most delicious muffins. When he handed them to Myrtle, he bowed.

The fairy Ethelinda was getting anxious. Punishments weren't supposed to work this way.

Rosella tried not to talk while she got ready for her betrothal, but her Royal Ladies-in-Waiting ignored her if she just pointed at things. They didn't yell at each other anymore, because they didn't want Prince Harold to hear, but that didn't stop them from fighting quietly.

When Rosella said, "I'll wear that gown," two amazon stones and an opal fell to the carpet. And the twelve Royal Ladies-in-Waiting went for the jewels, hitting and shoving each other.

So Rosella took the gown out of the closet herself and laid it out on her bed. Then she stood over it, marveling. It was silk, with an embroidered bodice. Its gathered sleeves ended in lace that would tickle her fingers delightfully. And the train was lace over silk, yards and yards of it.

"It's so pretty," she whispered. "It belongs in the sky with the moon and the stars."

Two pearls and a starstone fell into the deep folds of the gown's skirt. They were seen by a Royal Lady-in-Waiting who had taken a break from the fight on the carpet. She pounced on the gown.

The other Royal Ladies-in-Waiting heard the silk

rustle. They pounced too. In less time than it takes to sew on a button, the gown lay in tatters on the bed.

Rosella wanted to scream, but she was afraid to. Screaming might make bigger and better gems. Then she'd have to scream all the time. Besides, her throat was really starting to hurt. She cried instead.

The fairy Ethelinda was getting angry. Rewards weren't supposed to work this way.

Six

Rosella didn't mean to, but she dropped jewels on every gown in her princess wardrobe except one. And her Royal Ladies-in-Waiting ruined each of them. The one that was left was made of burlap and it was a size and a half too big. It didn't have a real train, but it did trail on the floor, because it was four inches too long.

Harold met Rosella in the palace's great hall, where the Chief Royal Councillor was going to perform the betrothal ceremony. The prince thought she looked pretty, with her brown wavy hair and her big gray eyes. But why had she picked the ugliest gown in the kingdom? It was big enough for her and a gorilla. All he said, though, was, "You look beautiful, honey bunch. Are you glad to be engaged?"

Rosella didn't know how to answer. Being engaged wasn't the problem, although marrying Harold might have its drawbacks. The problem was the jewels.

"Did you hear me, hon? I asked you a question." He raised his voice. "Are you happy, sweetheart?" He cupped his hand under her chin.

Rosella spoke through her teeth so the jewels wouldn't get out. "Everybody wants me to talk, but nobody listens to what I say."

"I'm listening, angel. Spit it out."

"I hate wild boar, and I don't want guards to stand around. . . ." There were so many jewels in her mouth that one popped out, a hyacinth.

Harold put it in his pocket. The orchestra started to play.

She couldn't keep all these stones in her mouth. She spit them into her hand and made a fist.

"We're supposed to hold hands," Harold whispered. "Give them to me. I'll take good care of them."

What difference did it make? She let him have them.

The ceremony began.

⚓ ⚓ ⚓

Myrtle sat on the edge of the well to eat her muffins. After she ate them and licked her fingers, she headed for the stationer's shop. When she got there, an earwig and a spider bought her enough party invitations for everyone in the village. At the bottom of each invitation she wrote, "Bring presents."

She gave out all the invitations, and everyone promised to come. Then she stopped at the tailor's shop, where she picked out a gown for the party. It was white silk with an embroidered bodice and a lace train.

She was in such a good mood, she even bought a gown for her mother.

The fairy Ethelinda was furious.

♣ ♣ ♣

At the end of the betrothal ceremony, the First Chancellor placed a golden tiara on Rosella's head. She wondered if she was a princess yet, or still just a princess-to-be.

"Some people want to meet you, honey," Harold said.

After a Royal Engagement, the kingdom's loyal

subjects were always allowed into the palace to meet their future princess.

The Royal Guards opened the huge wooden doors to the great hall. Rosella saw a line that stretched for three quarters of a mile outside the palace. Everyone in it had something to catch the jewels as they cascaded out of her mouth. Pessimists brought thimbles and egg cups. Optimists brought sacks and pillowcases and lobster pots.

The first subject Rosella met was a farmer. "How are you?" he said.

"Fine." A ruby chip fell into his pail.

That was all? His shoulders slumped.

Rosella took pity on him. She said, "Actually, my throat hurts, and this crown is giving me a headache."

He grinned as stones clattered against the bottom of his pail. Rosella asked him what he planned to do with the jewels.

"My old plow is worn out," he said. "I need a new one."

"Do you have enough now?" she said.

"Oh yes, Your Princess-ship. Thank you." He bowed and shook her hand.

Next in line was a woman whose skirt and blouse were as ragged as Rosella's had been yesterday. The woman wanted to buy a warm coat for the winter. Something about her made Rosella want to give her diamonds.

Rosella said, "Make sure your new coat is lined with fur. I think beaver is best." Diamond, she thought. Diamond, diamond.

But only one diamond came out, along with a topaz, some aquamarine stones, and some garnets. Thinking the name of the jewel didn't seem to make much difference. Anyway, the woman caught the stones in a threadbare sack and left happy.

A shoemaker came next, carrying a boot to catch the jewels. "What's your favorite flower?" he asked.

"Lilacs and carnations and daffodils." Rosella sang, wondering if singing would affect what came out—a diamond, a ruby, and a turquoise on the large side.

The shoemaker said he had been too poor to buy leather to make any more shoes. "But now," he said, "I can buy enough to fill my shop window."

Rosella smiled. "And peonies and poppies and

black-eyed Susans and marigolds and—"

She was starting to get the hang of it. Long vowels usually made precious jewels, while short vowels often made semiprecious stones. The softer she spoke, the smaller the jewels, and the louder the bigger. It really was a good thing she hadn't screamed at her Royal Ladies-in-Waiting.

"That's enough. Don't use them all up on me."

Rosella wished Harold would listen to this shoemaker. He could learn something.

Even though her throat hurt, she enjoyed talking to everybody. She liked her subjects! But why were so many of them poor?

Next was a boy who asked her to tell him a story. She made up a fable about a talkative parrot who lived with a deaf mouse. The boy listened and laughed in all the right places, and caught the jewels in his cap.

She smiled bravely and said hello to the next subject. Her throat hurt terribly.

Seven

The widow Pickering loved her new gown. She tried it on while Myrtle tried on her own new gown. The widow told Myrtle that she looked fantastic. Myrtle wrote that the new gown made her mother look twenty years younger.

They took off the gowns and hung them up so they wouldn't wrinkle. Then Myrtle went out into the yard to experiment. She hummed softly. A line of ants pushed between her lips. She hummed louder, and the ants got bigger. Even louder, and the ants got even bigger. She'd had no idea there were such big ants. These were as big as her big toe.

Enough ants. Myrtle opened her mouth wide and sang, "La, la, la, la. Tra lee tra la tra loo." Moths, fireflies, and ladybugs flew out.

She hummed again. This time worms and cater-pillars wriggled out. Hmmm. So she didn't always get ants by humming.

She tried speaking. "Nasty. Mean. Smelly. Rotten. Stupid. Loathsome." She giggled. "Vile. Putrid. Scabby. Mangy . . ."

They were crowding out—crawling, flitting, slith-ering, darting, wriggling, whizzing, oozing, flying, marching—escaping from Myrtle's mouth every way they could.

There were aphids, butterflies, mambas, lacewings, lynx spiders, midges, wolf snakes, gnats, mayflies, rhi-noceros vipers, audacious jumping spiders, bandy-bandy snakes, wasps, locusts, fleas, thrips, ticks, and every other bug and spider and snake you could think of.

Myrtle kept experimenting. She had a wonderful time, but she didn't figure out how to make a par-ticular snake or insect come out. All she learned was that the louder she got, the bigger the creature that came out.

After about an hour, she had worked up quite an appetite. So she and her mother went to the village

"THEY WERE CROWDING OUT—
CRAWLING, FLITTING, SLITHERING."

to have dinner at the inn. Dinner was free, because the innkeeper wanted to keep Myrtle from saying one single solitary word.

The fairy Ethelinda was scandalized.

⚓ ⚓ ⚓

During the betrothal banquet Harold noticed that Rosella's voice was fading. He noticed because all he got were tiny gems, hardly more than shavings. So he didn't make her say much. But he did make her drink wild-boar broth.

"It's the best thing for you, tootsie," he said when she made a face.

She gulped it down and hoped it would stay there. She picked at her string beans. "Why are your subjects so poor?" she whispered. A tiny sapphire and bits of amber fell onto the tablecloth.

Harold brushed the jewels into his hand. His betrothed was sweet, but she didn't know much. Subjects were always poor. "I wish they were richer too, cutie pie. Then I could tax them more."

"Maybe we can help them." A pearl fell into Rosella's mashed potatoes.

Harold dug it out with his fork and rinsed it off in his mulled wine. "Honey, you'll wear yourself out worrying about them. Take it easy. Relax a little."

She fell asleep over dessert. Royal Servants carried her to her bedchamber. But she woke up when the three Royal Guards took their places around her bed. Then she couldn't fall back to sleep.

Eight

Myrtle and the widow Pickering slept late the next morning. When they woke up, they strolled to the village. They stopped at the toymaker's shop for favors for the party guests. From the potter they ordered serving platters. The butcher promised them sausages and meat pies. By noon they had picked out everything for the party. Then they linked arms and sauntered home.

The fairy Ethelinda gnashed her teeth.

⚓ ⚓ ⚓

By morning Rosella's throat hurt worse than ever. She thought she had a fever, too. But her voice was stronger.

Breakfast was wild-boar steak and eggs. Before her

Royal Ladies-in-Waiting had taken ten bites, Harold sent for her.

He was waiting in the library. As soon as she went in, she became very scared. There were thousands of books, but they weren't what scared her. She liked books. There were four desks. That was fine, too. There were a dozen upholstered leather chairs, and they looked comfortable enough. A Royal Manservant and a Royal Maid were dusting. They were all right.

The terrifying sight was the fifteen empty chests lined up in front of one of the leather chairs.

"Sweetie pie," Harold said. "Am I glad to see you." He led her to the chair behind the empty chests. "Wait till I tell you my idea."

Rosella sat down.

"Did you have a good breakfast, cuddle bunch?"

It hurt too much to talk. She shook her head.

Harold was too excited to pay attention. "Good. Here's my idea. You've noticed how old and moldy this palace is?"

She shook her head.

"You haven't? Well, it is. The drawbridge creaks. The rooms are drafty. The cellars are full of rats.

41

The place should be condemned."

She didn't say anything. The palace looked fine to her.

"So I had a brainstorm. You didn't know you were marrying a genius, did you?"

She shook her head.

"This is brilliant. Listen. We're going to build a new castle. That's my idea. Picture it. Cream-colored stone. Marble everywhere. Hundreds of fountains. Taller towers than anybody ever heard of. Crocodiles *and* serpents in the moat. People will travel thousands of miles to see it. You'll be famous, sweetheart."

"Me?"

Harold caught the tiny ruby. "Yes, you. I can't build a palace on current revenues. We need your voice. The kingdom needs you. So just make sure they land in the chests, will you, sugar?"

She was silent.

"I know. You're wondering how you'll ever think of things to say to fill fifteen chests. That's why we're in the library. All you have to do is read out loud. Here." He pulled a book off a shelf. "This looks interesting. *The History of the Monarchy in the Kingdom of Biddle.*

That's us, love." He put the book in her lap. "You can read about our family."

She didn't open it. What could he do to her if she didn't talk? He could throw her in a dungeon. She wouldn't mind if he did. Bread and water would be better than wild boar. Then again, he could chop off her head, which would hurt her throat even more than it was hurting now.

"I know you're tired, darling. But after you fill these chests, you can take a vacation. You won't have to say a word." He got down on one knee. "Please, sweetheart. Pretty please."

He has his heart set on a new palace, Rosella thought. He'll be miserable if he doesn't get one, and it will be because of me. Rosella opened the book to the middle. I'm too kindhearted, she thought. She started reading, trying to speak around her sore throat. "The fourth son of King Beauregard the Hairy weighed seven pounds and eleven ounces at birth. He had a noodle-shaped birthmark on his left shoulder. He wailed for . . ."

A stream of jewels fell into the chest. Harold tiptoed out of the room.

Rosella went on reading. "The infant was named Durward. His first word, 'More,' proved him to be . . ." She was freezing. She looked up. The fire looked hot. ". . . proved him to be a true royal son. His tutors reported . . ." The room was spinning. ". . . reported that he excelled at archery, hunting . . ." What was wrong with this book? The letters were getting bigger and smaller. The lines of print were wavy. ". . . hunting, and milit—"

Rosella fainted and fell off her chair.

The Royal Manservant and Royal Maid rushed to the partly filled chest. They each grabbed a handful of jewels. Then the Royal Manservant ran to find Harold, while the Royal Maid used her apron to fan Rosella.

"Wake up, Your Highness. Please wake up," she cried.

Nine

The fairy Ethelinda was appalled. This was the last straw. She had to do something.

Harold was in the courtyard, practicing his swordplay. She materialized in front of him. She didn't bother to disguise herself, hoping he'd be terrified when he saw the works—all seven feet three inches of her, her fleshy pink wings, the shimmer in the air around her, the purple light she was always bathed in, her flashing wand.

"You're a fairy, right?" Harold said when he saw her. He didn't seem frightened.

"I am the fairy Ethelinda," she said, lowering her voice to a roar.

Harold grinned. "Pretty good guessing on my part, considering I've never met a fairy before."

"HAROLD WAS IN THE COURTYARD,
PRACTICING HIS SWORDPLAY."

"I am the one who made the jewels come out of Rosella's mouth."

Harold almost jumped up and down, he was so excited. "That was you? Really? Uh, say, Ethel . . . tell me, what did my sweetie pie do to make you do it?"

"My name is *Ethelinda*," the fairy boomed. "I rewarded her after she gave me a drink of well water."

"I can do that. That's a—"

"I'm not thirsty. Do you know that you're making poor Rosella miserable?"

"She's not miserable. She's a princess. She's deliriously happy."

Ethelinda tried a different approach. "Why do you want jewels so much?"

"You wouldn't want them?"

"Not if it was making my betrothed unhappy."

"How could she be unhappy? If I were in her shoes, I'd be delighted. She wouldn't be a princess today if I hadn't come along. She gets to wear a crown. She has nice gowns, Royal Ladies-in-Waiting. And me."

"You have to stop making her talk."

"But she has to talk. That's what makes *me* happy."

Ethelinda raised her wand. Prince Harold was one second away from becoming a frog. Then she lowered it. Her self-confidence was gone. If she turned him into a frog, he might figure out a way to make it better than being a prince. She certainly didn't want to reward him the way she'd rewarded Myrtle.

She didn't know what to do.

The Royal Manservant who'd seen Rosella faint finally reached the courtyard. He ran to Harold.

Ethelinda vanished.

⚓ ⚓ ⚓

Myrtle's party started at two o'clock. The schoolteacher arrived first. His present was a slate and ten boxes of colored chalk.

Myrtle opened one of the boxes. She wrote on the slate in green and orange letters, "Thank you. I'll let you know when I run out of chalk."

The baker came next. His cake was so big that it barely fit through the cottage doorway. The icing was chocolate. The decorations were pink and blue whipped cream. The writing on top said, "Happy Fourteen-and-Six-Weeks Birthday, Myrtle! Please Keep Quiet!"

The whole village came. Nobody wanted to take a chance on making Myrtle mad. The guests filled the cottage and the yard and the yards of the surrounding cottages. The widow thanked them all for coming. Myrtle collected her presents. She smiled when anyone handed her an especially big box.

The food was the finest anybody could remember. Myrtle ate so many poached quail eggs and roasted chestnuts that she almost got sick. After everybody ate, she opened her presents. There were hundreds of them. Her favorites were:

The framed sampler that read, "Speak to me only with thine eyes."

The bouquet of mums.

The music box that played "Hush, Little Baby."

The silver quill pen, engraved with the motto "The pen is mightier than the voice."

The parrot that sat on Myrtle's shoulder and repeated over and over, "Shut your trap. Shut your trap. Shut your trap."

The charm bracelet with the golden letters S, I, L, E, N, C, and E.

After all the presents were opened, everybody sang "Happy Birthday." Myrtle was so thrilled that she smiled and clapped her hands.

⚓ ⚓ ⚓

Rosella was gravely ill, and Harold was seriously frightened. Even under mounds of swansdown quilts, she couldn't stop shivering. She felt as if a vulture's claws were scratching at her throat and a carpenter hammering at her temples.

The Royal Physician was called in to examine her. When he was finished, he told Harold that she was very sick. He said her only hope of recovery lay in bed rest and complete silence. His fee for the visit was the jewels he collected when he listened to her chest and made her say "Aah" sixteen times.

Ten

Myrtle had a birthday party every week. She and the widow laughed and laughed at their silliness in wishing for jewels to come out of Myrtle's mouth. When Myrtle got bored between parties, she would speak into a big jar. Then she'd let the bugs and the snakes loose in the yard and make them race. She and her mother would have a grand time betting on the winners.

Rosella got better so slowly that Ethelinda's patience snapped. The evening after Myrtle's fourth party, Ethelinda materialized as herself in the widow's cottage. "I am the fairy Ethelinda, who rewarded your sister and punished you. You have to help Rosella," she thundered.

Myrtle sneered. "I do? I have to?"

A bull snake slithered under Ethelinda's gown. A gnat bit her wing.

"Ouch!" Ethelinda yelped.

"Be careful, dear," the widow told Myrtle. "You might make a poisonous snake."

"Yes, you have to help her," Ethelinda said. "Or I'll punish you severely."

Myrtle wrote on her slate, "I like your punishments."

"I can take your punishment away," Ethelinda said.

As fast as she could, Myrtle wrote, "What do I have to do?"

Ethelinda explained the problem.

"I can fix that," Myrtle wrote.

Ethelinda transported Myrtle to the palace, where Rosella was staring up at her lace bed canopy and wondering when her nighttime guards would arrive. As Ethelinda and Myrtle materialized, Ethelinda turned herself back into the old lady.

"I've brought your sister to help you, my dear," Ethelinda said.

Rosella stared at them. Myrtle would never help her. Myrtle had brought her slate with her. She wrote,

"Change clothes with me and hide under the covers."

Rosella didn't move. She wondered if she was delirious.

"Go ahead. Do it," Ethelinda said. "She won't hurt you."

Rosella nodded. She put on Myrtle's silk nightdress with the gold embroidery and slipped deep under the blankets. Myrtle got into Rosella's silk nightdress with the silver embroidery.

Myrtle climbed into Rosella's bed. She sat up and yodeled, long and loud. A hognose snake wriggled out of her mouth.

Harold heard her, even though he was at the other end of the palace. He started running, leaping, and skipping toward the sound. "She's better! She's well again!" he yelled. And how many jewels did that yodel make? he wondered.

Ethelinda made the snake disappear. Then she made herself invisible.

"Precious!" Harold said, coming through the door. He dashed to the bed. "The roses are back in your cheeks. Speak to me!"

"What roses?" Myrtle yelled as loud as she could.

"I feel terrible." The head of a boa constrictor filled her mouth.

Harold jumped back. "Aaaa! What's that?"

Rosella lifted a tiny corner of blanket so she could watch. The snake slithered out and wound itself around Myrtle's waist.

Myrtle grinned at Harold. "Do you like him? Should I name him after you?" Three hornets flew straight at him. One of them stung him on the nose. The other two buzzed around his head.

"Ouch! Wh-what's going on . . . h-honey pie? Th-that's a s-snake. Wh-where did the j-jewels go? Why are b-bugs and snakes coming out?"

This is fun, Myrtle thought. Who'd have thought I could scare a prince?

Poor Harold, Rosella thought. But it serves him right. He looks so silly. She fought back a giggle and wished she could make a bug come out of her mouth once in a while.

"I'm angry. This is what happens when I get angry." A scorpion stuck its head out of Myrtle's mouth.

"Yow! Why are you angry? At me? What did I do?"

"It's not so great being a princess," Myrtle yelled. "Nobody listens to me. All they care about are the jewels. You're the worst. It's all you care about, too. And I don't want to eat wild boar ever again. I hate wild boar."

The air was so thick with insects that Harold could hardly see. Snakes wriggled across the carpets. Snakes slithered up the sconces. Snakes oozed down the tapestries. A gigantic one hung from the chandelier, its head swaying slowly.

A milk snake slipped under the covers. It settled its clammy body next to Rosella. She wanted to scream and run. Instead, she bit her lip and stayed very, very still.

"Sweetheart, I'm sorry. Forgive me. Ouch! That hurt."

Myrtle screamed, "I'M NOT GOING TO TALK UNLESS I WANT TO!"

"All right. All right! You won't have to. And I'll listen to you. I promise." Something bit his foot all the way through his boot. He hopped and kicked to get rid of it. "Everyone will listen. By order of Prince Harold."

"AND PRINCESS ROSELLA," Myrtle yelled.

"And Princess Rosella," Harold echoed.

Myrtle lowered her voice. "Now leave me. I need my rest."

Eleven

After Harold left, Ethelinda made the snakes and bugs disappear. Rosella came out from under the covers.

"Thank you," Rosella told her sister. An emerald fell on the counterpane.

Myrtle snatched the jewel and said, "You're welcome." She snagged the fly before it got to Rosella's face. Then she crushed it in her fist.

"You've done a good deed," Ethelinda began.

Myrtle shook her head. "Don't reward me. Thanks, but no thanks." She let two cockroaches fall into the bed.

Ethelinda asked if Myrtle would help Rosella again if she needed it.

"Why should I?" Myrtle asked.

"I'll pay you," Rosella said.

Myrtle pocketed the two diamonds. Not bad. She'd get to frighten the prince again and get jewels for it, too. "Okay."

Myrtle and Rosella switched clothes again. Then Ethelinda sent Myrtle back home. When Myrtle was gone, Ethelinda said she had to leave too. She vanished.

Rosella sank back into her pillows. She didn't want Myrtle to help again, or even Ethelinda. She wanted to solve the problem of Harold and his poor subjects all by herself.

⚓ ⚓ ⚓

Harold didn't dare visit Rosella again that day. But he did command the Royal Servants to listen to her. So Rosella got rid of her nighttime guards. And she had her meal of poached quail eggs and roasted chestnuts at last.

She also ordered the Royal Ladies-in-Waiting to bring her a slate and chalk. From then on, she wrote instead of talking to them. She was tired of having them dive into her lap whenever she said anything.

And she had them bring her a box with a lock and a key. She kept the box and the slate by her side so she'd be ready when Harold came.

He showed up a week after Myrtle's visit. Rosella felt fine by then. She was sitting at her window, watching a juggler in the courtyard.

"Honey?" He poked his head in. He was ready to run if the room was full of creepy-crawlies. But the coast seemed clear, so he stepped in all the way. He was carrying a bouquet of daisies and a box of taffy. "All better, sweetheart?" He held the daisies in front of his face in case any hornets started flying.

He looks so scared, Rosella thought. She smiled to make him stop worrying.

He lowered the bouquet cautiously and placed it on a table. Then he sat next to her and looked her over. She seemed healthy. That silk nightdress was cute. Blue was a good color for her.

He hoped she wasn't feeling miserable anymore. Anyone who was going to marry him should be the happiest maiden in the kingdom. He still wanted her to talk up enough jewels for a new palace. Then, after that, he wouldn't mind a golden coach and a few other

"THEY SAT THERE, NOT SAYING ANYTHING."

items. But he wanted her to be happy, too.

They sat there, not saying anything.

"Oh, here," Harold said finally. He held out the bouquet and the candy.

She took them. "Thank you."

An opal hovered on her lip and tumbled out. Harold reached for it, but Rosella was faster. She opened her box and dropped in the opal. It clinked against the stones already in there. She snapped the box shut.

That was pretty selfish of her, Harold thought. He started to get mad, but then he thought of boa constrictors and hornets. He calmed down. "What's the box for, darling?"

"My jewels." A pearl came out this time. A big one. It went into the box too.

"Honey . . . Sweetie pie . . . What are you going to do with them?"

"Give them away. Your subjects need them more than we do."

"NO YOU DON'T!" Harold hollered. She couldn't! It was all right to give jewels away for the engagement ceremony. That was once in a lifetime, but she wanted to make a habit of it. "You can't give them away. I won't allow it."

Rosella wrote on her slate, "I'm trying not to get angry."

"No, no, don't get mad!" Harold started backing away. "But don't you want a new palace? I'll tell you what—we'll name a wing after you. It'll be the Rosella Wing. How do you like that?"

She shook her head. "This palace is beautiful. Look at it! It's wonderful."

All those gems going into the box! thought Harold. Wasted! If she gave them away, soon his subjects would be richer than he was. "Tell you what," Harold said. "We'll split fifty-fifty."

"I won't read a million books out loud just to fill up your treasure chests."

He counted as they fell. Two diamonds, three blood-stones, one hyacinth, and one turquoise.

He sighed. "All right, my love."

"All right, my love. Fifty-fifty." Rosella wanted to be fair. He had made her a princess, after all.

They shook hands. Then they kissed.

Epilogue

Myrtle never had to come to her sister's rescue ever again. The fifty-fifty deal worked out perfectly. Harold got his new palace and golden coach, eventually. And Rosella was happy talking to her subjects and making sure they had enough plows and winter coats and leather for making shoes. Also, she built them a new school and a library and a swimming pool.

In time she and Harold grew to love each other very much. Harold even stopped trying to steal the jewels from Rosella's wooden box while she was sleeping. And Rosella stopped counting them every morning when she woke up.

Myrtle and her mother went into the bug-and-snake-racing business. People came from twenty kingdoms to watch Myrtle's races. They'd bet beetles against spiders or rattlers against pythons or grasshoppers against garter snakes. The widow would call the races, and Myrtle would take the bets. The whole village got rich from the tourist trade. And Myrtle became truly popular, which annoyed her.

Ethelinda grew more careful. Myrtle was her last mistake. Nowadays when she punishes people, they stay punished. And when she rewards them, they don't get sick.

And they all lived happily ever after.

The End.

Rosella's Song

Oh, January is the first month.

Sing hey nonny January-o!

Oh, February is the cold month.

Sing hey nonny February-o!

Oh, March is the windy month.

Sing hey nonny March-o!

Oh, April is the rainy month.

Sing hey nonny April-o!

Oh, May is the lovely month.

Sing hey nonny May-o!

Oh, June is the flower month.

Sing hey nonny June-o!

Oh, July is the hot month.

Sing hey nonny July-o!

Oh, August is the berry month.

Sing hey nonny August-o!

Oh, September is the red-leaf month.

Sing hey nonny September-o!

Oh, October is the scary month.

Sing hey nonny October-o!

Oh, November is the harvest month.

Sing hey nonny November-o!

Oh, December is the last month.

Sing hey nonny December-o!

The Princess Test

To Martha Garner,

who told me to be sweet.

—G.C.L.

One

Once upon a time, in the village of Snettering-on-Snoakes in the Kingdom of Biddle, a blacksmith's wife named Gussie gave birth to a baby girl. Gussie and her husband, Sam, named the baby Lorelei, and they loved her dearly.

Lorelei's smile was sweet and her laughter was music. But as an infant she smiled only four times and laughed twice. The rest of the time she cried.

She cried when her porridge was too hot or too cold or too salty or too bitter or too sweet. She cried when her bathwater was too hot or too cold or too wet or not wet enough. She cried when her diaper was scratchy or smelly or not folded exactly right. She cried when her cradle was messy or when her mother forgot to make it with hospital corners. She cried whenever anything was not perfectly perfect.

Sam and Gussie did their best to make her happy. Lorelei was the only village baby with satin sheets and velvet diapers. She was the only one whose milk came from high-mountain yaks. And she was the only one who ate porridge made from two parts millet mixed with one part buckwheat. But still she cried.

She cried less as she learned to talk.

Then one day Lorelei said, "Father dearest and Mother dearest, I'm terribly sorry for crying so much. You have been too good to me."

Gussie said, "Oh honey, it's all right."

Sam said, "Gosh, we thought you were the cutest, best baby in this or any other kingdom."

Lorelei shook her head. "No, I was difficult. But I shall try to make it up to you. And now that I can explain myself, everything will be much better." She smiled. Then she sneezed. And sneezed again. She smiled shakily. "I fear I have a cold."

From then on, Lorelei stopped crying. She didn't stop being a picky eater, and she didn't stop needing everything to be just so. She just stopped crying about it.

"SHE SMILED SHAKILY. 'I FEAR I HAVE A COLD.'"

Instead, Lorelei started being sick and having accidents.

If a child in the village of Snettering-on-Snoakes had a single spot, Lorelei caught the measles. If a child two villages and a mountain away had the mumps, Lorelei caught them, and the flu besides.

She loved the other children, and they liked her well enough. But if she played tag with them, she was sure to trip and skin her knee or her elbow or her chin. When they played hopscotch, she always twisted her ankle. Once, when she tried to jump rope, she got so tangled up that Gussie had to come and untie her.

When Lorelei turned fourteen, Gussie died. Sam and Lorelei were heartbroken. Sam swore never to marry again because Gussie was the sweetest wife anybody could ever have.

"Besides," he added, "all the old tales say that stepmothers are mean to their stepdaughters. You'll never have to worry about that, Lorelei honey."

Two

$\mathcal{S}$am knew that Lorelei couldn't cook and clean for him and be her own nurse too. Besides, he'd be leaving soon for his annual trip to shoe the horses of the Earl of Pildenue, and someone would have to take care of Lorelei while he was gone. So he looked around for a housekeeper.

A wench named Trudy had helped the shoemaker's family when their twins were born. The shoemaker said that Trudy was a hard worker, so Sam hired her. Trudy wondered why a blacksmith with a grown daughter needed a housekeeper, but she took the job.

As soon as Trudy walked in the door, Lorelei ran to her, stumbled, and fell into Trudy's arms.

"Dear Trudy, I'll do anything to help you. To the outer limits of my meager ability."

Nobody had ever called Trudy "dear" before. So she thought this could be a pretty cushy spot, even if she understood only one word in ten that the lass said. But then again, if the girl wanted to help, why were the dirty dishes piled as high as a horse's rear end? Trudy shrugged and pumped water into the sink. "Here, lass. You can start on these."

"Oh, good!" Lorelei took the soap and started to scrub a plate.

Trudy looked around for a mop.

"Oh dear," Lorelei said.

"What's amiss?"

Lorelei raised her arms out of the soapy water. Trudy was horrified. The girl's arms and hands were covered with a bright-red rash.

"Does this happen whenever you wash a dish?" Trudy asked.

"I don't know. I've never washed one before."

Never washed a dish! Her poor dead mother had let her get away with that? Had the woman mistaken her daughter for a princess?

"Mother kept the unguents and the bandages in the hutch," Lorelei said.

Trudy opened the hutch door. There were enough potions and herbs and simples to set up shop as a wisewoman.

"That one. There." Lorelei pointed to a big jar.

Trudy spread the salve over Lorelei's rash.

"It has to be wrapped in clean linen." Lorelei pointed again.

Trudy wrapped up Lorelei's arms—three times. The first time the bandages were too tight. The next time they were too loose. An hour passed before Lorelei said they were just right.

At last! Trudy thought, Her majesty is satisfied.

"The dressing has to be changed every two hours," Lorelei said. "I'm sorry to be such a bother."

Trudy frowned. It wasn't exactly her highness's fault, but over an hour had gone by and the dishes were still dirty. The floor hadn't been mopped, and there was a mountain of laundry in the basket. She'd be working half the night to get it all done.

⚓ ⚓ ⚓

Trudy worked half the night that night and every night. For a month she took off bandages and put on bandages. When the rash was gone, Lorelei offered to help again.

Trudy hadn't been able to do any spinning because of all the bandaging. Surely, she thought, her majesty can't come to grief spinning. "Can you help me with the spinning?"

Lorelei smiled happily. Gussie had never let her near the spinning wheel. She knew exactly what to do, though, because she'd watched her mother so often. She sat down at the wheel and got started.

Trudy nodded. There. She began to dust.

"Oh dear."

Trudy turned around. Lorelei had stabbed herself in the hand with the spindle, and blood was pouring onto the cottage's wooden floor. Trudy ran for the bandages.

While Trudy bandaged her, Lorelei apologized at least a thousand times. After that, Trudy spent an hour scrubbing blood off the wooden floor and wondering what the bungling ninny was good for.

Not much, Trudy soon discovered. Lorelei could hang laundry on the line, and she could make a bed neatly. But the only thing she was really good at was embroidery. And Trudy had no need for embroidery. What she needed was to scream, long and loud.

Every day Trudy got madder and madder. While she washed Lorelei's satin sheets, her ladyship would be sitting at her ease, embroidering by the window. As Trudy kneaded Lorelei's special millet-buckwheat bread, the lazy thing would be lying in bed because her poor little throat hurt. Or her poor little left eyebrow. Or her poor little big toe.

Then came the joyous moment when Trudy thought of doing Lorelei in. Cooking her highness's goose. Rubbing her pampered self o-u-t. *Out!* Trudy started whistling.

Lorelei looked up from embroidering the outline of a potato on one of Sam's breeches. She smiled. "I'm so glad you're happy here, Trudy."

"Oh, I am, lass, I am. Happier every minute."

Three

It was lunchtime in the nearby court of the king and queen of Biddle. Queen Hermione rang her little bell to let the Royal Servants know they could bring out the first course.

The Chief Royal Lunchtime Serving Maid carried a platter heaped with crab cakes into the royal dining room. King Humphrey helped himself to a tiny crab cake. Queen Hermione helped herself to a tiny crab cake. Prince Nicholas took a dozen or so crab cakes and started eating.

King Humphrey tasted his crab cake. Queen Hermione tasted her crab cake. They shook their heads. Queen Hermione rang her bell again. The Chief Royal Lunchtime Serving Maid stepped up to the royal table.

"I'm so sorry," Queen Hermione said. "These crab

cakes taste a bit too fishy to me."

"We beg to differ or disagree," the king boomed. "They're not fishy enough."

"Crab isn't a fish," Prince Nicholas said, chewing happily. "My compliments to the chef."

"Please bring grapefruit instead," the queen said.

The Chief Royal Lunchtime Serving Maid removed the platter. On her way into the kitchen she passed a counter where the royal lunch was laid out. There were platters of crusty beef Wellington, creamed potatoes, and asparagus in mustard sauce, and there was a basket of poppy seed popovers. And two plates of grapefruit sections, poached eggs, and dry toast.

At a long table the Royal Servants waited for their lunch. The Chief Royal Lunchtime Serving Maid handed the platter of crab cakes to the Chief Royal Steward at the head of the table. He took four or five cakes and passed the plate to the Chief Royal House-keeper on his right.

"There would be more for us if the prince didn't eat so much," the Chief Royal Undergardener com-plained.

"Hush," the Chief Royal Housekeeper said. "We're lucky to serve two such finicky rulers. My cousin

Mabel doesn't fare half so well at the Earl of Pildenue's castle. The earl and his family adore their food, adore their clothes, adore their furniture. She never gets anything."

⚓ ⚓ ⚓

Back in Snettering-on-Snoakes, Lorelei ate her lunch of grapefruit, poached eggs, and dry toast, and patted her mouth with an embroidered napkin. Then she went out to hang embroidered laundry on the embroidered clothesline.

While she worked, she thought about her mother and Trudy. Her mother had been so good to her. And Trudy was too. They both worked so hard. She hadn't helped her mother much, or Trudy, even though she always wanted to.

Trudy looked tired sometimes, although she never complained. Gussie must have been tired too. But no matter how tired she might have been, her mother had always had a kiss and a hug for Lorelei. And even if the hugs had made Lorelei a little black and blue, she would have given anything to have them back again.

She wiped away a tear with the embroidered toe of Sam's hose.

Prince Nicholas, riding by, saw the tear. He had gone out after lunch to get some fresh air. As soon as he had turned into the lane, he'd seen Lorelei. She looked pretty in the distance. As he got closer, she was still pretty. Not a raving beauty, but definitely pretty. Light-brown hair. Ordinary color, but thick and wavy. Nose a little too big. But her eyes were big too. Enormous. And she had roses in her cheeks. You didn't see roses in the cheeks of the noble and stuck-up ladies at court.

Then he saw she was crying! A corner of his heart that had never been touched before was touched. He leaped off his steed. "Maiden!" he cried. "You weep!"

Lorelei turned and knocked over the laundry basket. Embroidered petticoats and tunics and bodices danced across the small muddy yard.

Prince Nicholas vaulted over the low fence and helped Lorelei gather up the wash. He picked up one of Sam's shirts, embroidered with three-legged stools. The stitchery was masterful. But why three-legged stools?

"LORELEI TURNED AND KNOCKED OVER
THE LAUNDRY BASKET."

He asked, "Maiden, why were you crying? Perhaps I can be of service."

Lorelei blushed. He wasn't that handsome, but there was something regal about him. Who was he? "I was missing my mother, kind sir."

"Your mother is . . ."

"She died." Lorelei smiled bravely and gathered up the last item of laundry, a petticoat embroidered with tiny teakettles.

The poor maiden was an orphan, Nicholas thought. Or half of one if her father was alive. "You have my most sincere sympathy, maiden." He wanted to say more but couldn't think of anything else.

Lorelei smiled. "Thank you, kind sir." He was nice!

She had a wonderful smile. He found himself stammering. "Er . . . I am P-Prince N-Nicholas."

He was a prince! She swept him a curtsy. "I am Lorelei."

Inside, Trudy glanced up from her washtub. Look at her highness out there, she thought, passing the time with a young lord. Not for long, your ladyship. She hummed and danced a little jig. Not for long, hey-ho! Not for long, tra-la!

Four

When Nicholas got back to the castle, King Humphrey summoned him to the throne room. As usual it was full of courtiers and subjects. King Humphrey had just settled an argument between two farmers over a cow. When he saw Nicholas, the king ordered everyone to leave. The only ones left were the king, the queen, the prince, and the Chief Royal Window Washer, who was cleaning the stained-glass windows.

"Son," King Humphrey boomed. "We are growing old or advancing in years. We should like to abdicate. But before we do, you must wed or get married."

Nicholas thought of Lorelei and his heart started to race. "I just met—"

"We must find you a true princess," Queen Hermione interrupted. "The descendent of a long line of royalty. A noble maiden, with . . ."

That eliminates Lorelei, Nicholas thought. Her pretty, rosy cheeks alone would rule her out.

"We've devised a test," the king said. "Or an examination."

"But what if I don't love the true princess?"

"You'll love her," Queen Hermione said. "She'll be just right for you."

No she won't! thought Nicholas.

"You'll make yourself love or adore her," King Humphrey roared. "Or we'll abdicate in favor of Archduke Percival."

Nicholas hated the archduke. Percy threw his servants into the moat if they did something wrong or if he felt like it. He would be a terrible king.

"Would you like to hear the test, dear?" the queen asked.

Nicholas nodded.

"When a maiden arrives who claims to be a true princess," Queen Hermione said, "we shall give her a bouquet."

The king guffawed. "But amidst all the fragrant or sweet-smelling flowers, there will be a sprig or small bunch of parsley. And that's not a flower."

Nicholas wondered what parsley had to do with being a princess.

"The true princess will know," the queen said. "She will pluck that parsley right out of her bouquet."

"That's the test?"

"Certainly not," Queen Hermione said. "There's more. We shall serve her a salad. A beautiful salad."

"Except," King Humphrey said, chuckling, "right in the middle, there will be a bit—"

"A speck—" the queen interrupted.

"The merest fleck. We don't want to hurt or injure the maiden. There will be a fleck of uncooked or raw noodle."

"The true princess will find it!" Queen Hermione announced.

What did parsley and noodles have to do with being a kind and just ruler? Nicholas listened in amazement to the rest of the test. There would be a trial in every course of the banquet. Also, the poor princess would be given a gown with a skirt that was a tint lighter than the bodice. She'd have to notice. She'd be shown a tapestry and would have to find the single missing stitch.

Lorelei might pass that one, Nicholas thought.

Every inch of the princess would be measured. Her waist had to be tiny. Her hands and feet had to be small, although her fingers had to be long. Her big toe had to be longer than her index toe. She had to be tall, but not a giant. And so on.

"But the final test will be the most important one," Queen Hermione said.

"There's more?" Nicholas said.

King Humphrey nodded solemnly. Then he nodded again.

"She will sleep in a guest bedroom," the queen said. "Her bed will be piled with twenty soft mattresses."

"She'll fall off!" Nicholas said. "She'll hurt—"

"A princess does not fall," the queen said. She went on. "Each mattress will be filled with the finest swans' feathers. But under the bottom mattress we will place a pea. If she sleeps well, she is no true princess!"

King Humphrey agreed. "If she sleeps or slumbers well, she is no true princess!"

⚓ ⚓ ⚓

The Chief Royal Chambermaid heard about the pea test from the Chief Royal Window Washer. It made her curious, so she got a pea from the Chief Royal

Cook. A dried pea, because they couldn't have meant a fresh one, which would just squoosh flat.

The Chief Royal Chambermaid made everything ready, just as it would be for the princess. One pea. Twenty mattresses. And a ladder.

She climbed up. The bed was sooo soft. It was delicious. Pea? She couldn't feel any pea. With twenty mattresses under her, she doubted she would feel a watermelon. She didn't think anybody could feel the pea—true princess, fake princess, or any other kind.

The Chief Royal Chambermaid climbed down and yanked off a few mattresses. Then she climbed back up. She still couldn't feel the pea. She pulled off more mattresses and tried again. Nothing.

She took off all the mattresses except the bottom one, but she still couldn't feel anything. She checked under the mattress. There it was. Well, she was no princess. Maybe a true princess could feel a pea under one or two mattresses. But under twenty? Not on your life.

Five

Sam got ready for his trip to the earldom of Pildenue. The earl was his only noble customer. Sam made enough from this one job to keep Lorelei in silk kirtles and embroidery thread for a year.

He said a long farewell to Lorelei in front of their cottage. "Be sure you wear your shawl at night, honey."

"I will, Father."

"Be sure she does, Trudy. I don't want her to get sick."

"Yes, Master," Trudy said. Would that be a good way to bump her off? Let her catch cold and die?

"And make her eat enough, Trudy. You have to keep your strength up, sweetie pie."

"Yes, Master," Trudy said. Should she starve

Lorelei? No. It would take too long.

"Here, sweet. Give your old daddy a kiss."

Lorelei hugged him. "I'll miss you, Father. Hurry home."

Sam climbed up to the seat of his wagon. He flapped the reins, and the old mare started to trot.

Lorelei wiped away a tear. She turned to Trudy. "We'll just have to keep each other company." She sniffled. "We'll have a lovely time, won't we?"

"Yes, lass." Yes indeed!

⚓ ⚓ ⚓

King Humphrey wrote a proclamation to announce the search for a real princess.

"Hear ye! Hear ye! Or listen well! Insofar and Inasmuch as We, King Humphrey, Supreme Ruler and Monarch of the Kingdom and Monarchy of Biddle . . ."

The king paused here. But there was no synonym for Biddle, so he went on.

". . . Wish to Abdicate Our Throne in Favor of Our Son and Heir, the Noble and Royal Prince Nicholas. And Insofar and Inasmuch as We

Stipulate and Require . . ."

And so on. The next important part came at the very end. ". . . and Said Princess Must Satisfy Us, King Humphrey, Supreme . . ." Blah blah blah. ". . . That She Is in Her Person and Her Self a Completely and Utterly True Princess. Our Judgment on This Matter or in This Respect Shall Be Final and Without Appeal."

Below that King Humphrey signed *King Humphrey or Supreme Ruler of Biddle*, as was his habit. The Royal Seal was affixed, and the proclamation was complete. And finished, too.

Except for one thing. The king wanted a portrait of Prince Nicholas to go with the proclamation. He sent for his Chief Royal Artist and Portrait Maker.

"My son or heir isn't a bad-looking boy, is he?" King Humphrey asked the artist. "There's nothing wrong with his looks, is there?"

"Oh no, Sire. Not in the slightest." The Chief Royal Artist and Portrait Maker thought the prince was ordinary-looking. Nothing special.

"The prince has to look handsome in his portrait or picture," the king said. "That way a true princess

95

will want and desire to come."

"I understand, sire." Smaller ears. Straighter mouth. Broader shoulders. He could do that.

Nicholas wanted to look as ugly as possible in his portrait. He wanted every princess who saw it to say, "Ugh. Who would want to marry *him*?" Because if no princesses showed up, he might be able to convince the king and queen to let him marry Lorelei.

So he squinted. He squirmed. He mussed his hair. He let his mouth hang open. He drooled. He borrowed Queen Hermione's makeup and drew a big black mole on his chin.

It made no difference. The Chief Royal Artist and Portrait Maker was a master craftsman. In the portrait Prince Nicholas' chin (without a mole) was lifted majestically. His eyes had a piercing look. A hint of a smile played around his mouth. His shoulders were broad. His mouth wasn't lopsided. His ears were perfect. Also, the Chief Royal Artist and Portrait Maker waved Nicholas' hair and thickened his eyelashes. Princesses would fall in love with those eyelashes. Guaranteed.

When all was ready, scribes copied the proclamation.

"THE SEARCH WAS ON."

Lesser Royal Artists and Portrait Makers copied the portrait. Messengers were dispatched to kingdoms near and far.

The search was on.

Six

Trudy thought about how to do Lorelei in. She could hit her over the head with the frying pan. Or strangle her with the embroidered clothesline. Or drag her to the village square and push her out of the clock tower. Any one of those would be lots of fun. But she'd be caught. The dopey villagers liked Lorelei.

It should be easy to finish her off, Trudy reasoned. After all, her highness was in bed sick or hurt three times a week without anybody doing anything to her. Why, she could murder herself one of these days without Trudy's having to lift a finger! Hmm. Now that was an idea.

The morning after Sam left, Trudy announced that she didn't feel well. "You'll have to do the housework today, lass," Trudy said. "I'm not up to it."

Lorelei would wash the dishes and she'd get that rash again. But today Trudy would be too sick to put on the salve. So Lorelei would swell up like a balloon and *POP!* And nobody would think it was Trudy's fault.

"Oh dear. Does your stomach ache?"

Trudy nodded.

"Oh dear. Does your forehead pulse?"

Trudy nodded.

"Your throat. Is it hard to swallow?"

Trudy nodded.

Lorelei clapped her hands. "Then I know just what to do. You've been so good to me, dear Trudy. And now I can help you." She threw open the door to the hutch and pulled out strangely shaped bottles and odd bundles of herbs.

"I used to get what you have," Lorelei said. "Mother made me well in a jiffy." She dumped whatever was in the bottles and bundles into a pot. Then she hung the pot on a hook in the fireplace.

Soon a sharp odor filled the room. Trudy's eyes watered. The hairs in her nose felt like they were burning.

"Doesn't it smell wonderful?" Lorelei asked. "I

always feel better when I smell the steam. In a few minutes you'll drink the broth and be well again, dear Trudy."

She was going to have to *drink* that slop? Trudy jumped up. "I feel much better. Fine. Really." She poured the disgusting brew on the fire. Stinky smoke billowed out. "You're a good wisewoman. You've cured me already." Trudy opened the cottage door and the windows. She could have been killed!

She started on the chores. What else could she do? Hmm. "Lass?"

"Yes, Trudy?"

"I'm off to the market. While I'm gone, would you like to try the spinning wheel again?"

"Oh yes!"

"I won't be long. Be careful with the spindle." Trudy shut the door behind her and sauntered down the lane. Her ladyship would stab herself again. By the time Trudy got back, Lorelei would have bled to death.

The market was busy. Trudy gossiped with the other shoppers. She told the peddlers what was wrong with their goods. She even bought herself a pink hair ribbon. Then she strolled back to the blacksmith's cottage. What a delightful day it was!

She opened the door. No, it was a terrible day! Lorelei wasn't bleeding. Not even a drop. The only thing that was hurt was the spinning wheel. It looked like a giant spider had spun a web all over it. It would take days to untangle the mess.

Lorelei was crying. "Oh, Trudy! I'm sorry. I wanted to have yards and yards of beautiful linen finished when you got back. You must be so disappointed in me."

Lorelei couldn't understand what Trudy was saying. It sounded something like "Argul! Gloog! Blub!" Trudy yanked open the cottage door and slammed it behind her. She stood on the doorstep, panting. She had to get a grip on herself. She couldn't let that little . . . that little good-for-nothing fancy *idiot* do this to her.

She had to plan it out better. She had plenty of time. Two months before Sam came home. Plenty of time.

Lorelei was as good as dead.

Seven

A month went by and no one arrived at the court of Biddle to take the princess test. Queen Hermione smiled knowingly. She said the young ladies were getting ready, having gowns made, making themselves beautiful for their prince.

Making themselves as princessy as possible, Nicholas thought. I want Lorelei! He wanted to cry.

Every day he rode to her lane in the village of Snettering-on-Snoakes. He spent hours watching the smoke curl out of her chimney. He didn't even have to see her. Just seeing the smoke was enough.

But sometimes he did see her, sitting at her window, embroidering. He'd wonder what she was sewing. Buckets? Doorknobs? Galoshes? He thought his heart would break in two pieces.

One day Lorelei was outside, picking roses from the bush outside the cottage door. She turned when she heard the clatter of his horse's hooves. It was that nice prince again, she thought. What was his name? Nicholas. A nice name. She curtsied.

Nicholas jumped off his horse. He bowed. What could he say to her? "Er . . . hello. Er . . . hello, maid Lorelei."

She smiled. "Hello, Your Highness."

"Fine weather we're having." He wished he could think of something more interesting to say.

"I think the clouds mean rain." Why couldn't she think of something more interesting to say? He probably knew a hundred princesses who could make fascinating conversation.

"Those roses are pretty. Did you plant them?"

Inside the cottage Trudy was cleaning the stove. She saw Lorelei through the window and wished the sluggard would prick herself with a poisoned thorn. She wished that the young lord talking to Lorelei were a highwayman who would kidnap her. Then he'd have to clean up after her and bandage her. Then she'd be his problem.

Hmm . . . Trudy thought, that's it! That's the way to get rid of her, once and for all.

⚓ ⚓ ⚓

The very next day a princess showed up at King Humphrey's court. She was Princess Cordelia from the nearby kingdom of Kulornia.

King Humphrey himself helped her down from her carriage.

She was good-looking. The king didn't have his tape measure with him, but she seemed tall enough. And her hands looked the right size.

Queen Hermione smiled. The maiden looked promising.

Prince Nicholas frowned and bowed. He could tell already. He didn't like Cordelia.

"Thank you." She curtsied. "Well, well, well. Here I am. We made good time getting here. We only stopped three times on the road. Traffic wasn't bad. Dandy courtyard you have here, Humphrey. Hello, Nicky. I see they exaggerated on your portrait. I expected that, so don't worry about it. They always do it in the marriage game. Well, well. Dandy courtyard . . ."

Queen Hermione looked at her husband. They had forgotten to put in a test for the art of conversation.

King Humphrey looked at his wife. They had forgotten to put in a test for talking your head off or never shutting up.

Nicholas looked at the sky. Nicky! He mustn't scream. He didn't have to marry anybody yet.

The king snapped his fingers. The Chief Royal Bouquet Maker stepped forward. He presented a bouquet to Princess Cordelia.

Let her not find the parsley, Nicholas prayed.

Let her not find the parsley or herb, the king prayed.

Let her not find the parsley, the queen prayed.

"Well, well, well. You folks sure know how to roll out the red carpet. There's nothing like a bunch of flowers to brighten things up. Take a dull tower room and—"

"Would you like us to put them in water, my dear?" Queen Hermione asked. If she said yes, it would be all over.

"Sure. Wouldn't want them to go limp and croak right in—"

"We're so glad you had a comfortable journey," King Humphrey interrupted firmly. "We hope or desire that it will be even better going the other way. Thank you so much for coming." He handed her back into the carriage and slapped the horses to get them moving quickly or rapidly

Princess Cordelia stuck her head out the window. "Well! What did I do? I thought we were getting along just fine. When you issue a . . ."

The three of them went back into the castle. They could hear Cordelia yelling till the heavy doors thudded shut behind them.

Eight

On the same day that the talkative Princess Cordelia was thrown out of Biddle, Trudy perfected her plan. She would lose Lorelei, plain and simple. And whoever found her would have to keep her—finders keepers. Trudy giggled.

"Lass," Trudy said. "What's the name of that herb you like in your tea sometimes?"

"Hyssop?"

"That's the one. We're fresh out of it, and there's none in the market."

"That's all right." Lorelei smiled bravely. "I can do without."

"But I don't want you to, sweet. I want you to be happy, honey lamb."

"You're so good to me."

Hah! "Tim, the spice peddler, told me where it grows in the forest. I thought we could harness your dad's mule and go there tomorrow. We'll have a picnic."

"What fun!"

Hooray! Trudy thought. The bumbling ninny would never find her way home from the middle of the forest.

⚓ ⚓ ⚓

The next day princesses arrived at the castle in droves. They came in carriages drawn by horses, by camels, by oxen. One even came in a carriage drawn by crocodiles. And another arrived in a hot-air balloon. The courtyard was clogged with animals and carriages and princesses. The Royal Guards got tired of raising and lowering the drawbridge. They decided to leave it lowered till the prince announced his engagement.

There were too many princesses to test one by one. So the king and queen decided to test them all together.

Nicholas looked them over. Some were too short. Some were too tall. Some were too thin. Some were too fat. They'd all fail the measurement test. But the rest seemed about right. The most beautiful princess was the one who'd come in the carriage pulled by crocodiles. She had huge purple eyes and a slow smile. She gave Nicholas the shivers. He kept feeling she didn't want to marry him—she really wanted to roast him and eat him with cream sauce.

⚓ ⚓ ⚓

In the forest Lorelei finished weaving a daisy chain. She was in a small clearing, sitting on an embroidered blanket, a velvet embroidered blanket, of course. The only kind that didn't make her itchy.

Trudy was hunting for hyssop, the herb for Lorelei's tea.

"Do you see any?" Lorelei called.

"Not yet. Eat your lunch. I'll be there soon."

Lorelei opened the picnic basket. Trudy's voice sounded faraway. Lorelei bit into her cucumber sandwich with the crusts cut off. "Trudy!" she called. "Come back. You must be hungry."

"Soon. I think I see something."

Lorelei could hardly hear the words. It was too bad that Trudy couldn't enjoy this beautiful day. The spice

"LORELEI FINISHED WEAVING A DAISY CHAIN."

peddler should have drawn a map showing exactly where the hyssop grew. Lorelei finished her lunch and leaned back on the blanket. Such sweet puffy white clouds. She closed her eyes. In a few minutes she was asleep.

Trudy led Leonard the mule along the trail next to the stream. Lorelei hadn't called in a while. It was safe to stop. Trudy tied Leonard to a tree and took the extra lunch out of his saddlebag. She kicked off her shoes and sat on a rock with her feet dangling in the cool water. She bit into her sandwich. Sausages and peppers. Her favorite. This was peace.

⚓ ⚓ ⚓

Prince Nicholas couldn't stand being around all these princesses for another minute. He saddled his horse and rode to Snettering-on-Snoakes. He had to see Lorelei.

But she wasn't there. Her cottage was empty.

⚓ ⚓ ⚓

The first drops of rain woke Lorelei. The sky was dark.

"Trudy?"

A roll of thunder drowned her out. The drops came down harder. They were huge.

"Trudy? Do you hear me?"

Had Trudy come back and eaten her lunch while she was asleep? Lorelei opened the basket. No. Trudy's sausage-and-peppers sandwich was still there. Trudy is lost! Lorelei thought. Poor Trudy. She must be terrified.

Lightning lit the sky. Were you supposed to get under a tree when there was lightning? Or stay away from trees?

At least she'd be drier under a tree. Lorelei jumped up and folded the blanket neatly. Then she took the picnic basket and ran under a tall maple.

She stayed under the tree for an hour. Every few minutes she called Trudy, but there was never an answer. The sky grew darker. Storm dark, but also night dark. Lorelei's stomach rumbled delicately. Time for dinner.

She had to find Trudy. It was her responsibility because she was Trudy's mistress. She had never felt so full of purpose before. She had to find Trudy and

Leonard the mule and get them home safely. She'd go to the stream first. The last time she'd heard Trudy's voice, it had come from there.

The stream was across the clearing and straight ahead, through a stand of trees. Lorelei stepped into the clearing and was drenched instantly. Oh well, she thought. It was only water.

"Trudy! Stay where you are. I'm coming." She didn't want poor Trudy to have one second more of terror than she had to.

As the water soaked into them, Lorelei's skirts got heavier and heavier and dragged more and more. It was hard to walk, but she had to do it.

"Trudy! I'm coming!"

Where was the stream? She should have reached it by now.

"Leonard?" Maybe the mule would hee-haw and she'd find him. Then she could ride him and find Trudy more quickly. She pushed past bushes and over fallen logs.

Two hours passed. Lorelei still hadn't found Leonard, Trudy, or the stream. She was hungry and chilled. She sneezed almost as often as she took a breath. She

114

couldn't get sick, not now when Trudy needed her.

Finally Lorelei sat on a tree stump and cried between sneezes. She had to admit it. Trudy was lost. Leonard was lost. And she was lost.

Nine

By dinnertime the flood of princesses had slowed to a trickle. Around ten o'clock it stopped. Seventy-nine princesses had come.

Queen Hermione set aside a wing of the castle just for them. Tonight they would sleep in ordinary beds with only one mattress and no pea. Tomorrow the tests would begin. Tomorrow night would be the final exam for those who had passed all the other tests. The mattress and pea test. The test that the Chief Royal Chambermaid was sure nobody could pass.

Prince Nicholas was beside himself. What was he going to do? And where was Lorelei?

⚓ ⚓ ⚓

Lorelei was flat on her face in the forest. She had tripped over a tree root, and she was too tired to get up.

Too tired to do anything except sneeze.

But she had to get back to the village and form a search party. She stood and picked up the picnic basket and blanket. Her gown and face were covered with mud and dead leaves. Well, the rain would clean off her face. And the gown didn't matter, since she hadn't had a chance to embroider anything on it yet.

She heard something. She stood still and fought back a sneeze. There it was again. A snuffling noise. Trudy! She opened her mouth to yell. But wait. What if it wasn't Trudy. What if it was—

Lorelei had never climbed a tree in her life. But she climbed one now. One second she was on the ground. The next she was twelve feet up.

A bear crashed through the bushes. She sneezed. Oh no! He was going to find her!

But he passed right by, in a big hurry. He didn't even look up. He was probably going to his nice warm cave. Lucky bear.

Lorelei climbed down from the tree and stumbled on. "Achoo!" Hang on, Trudy, she thought. Hang on. I'm coming.

⚓ ⚓ ⚓

Nicholas couldn't sleep. He paced up and down in his room. He didn't want to marry anyone but Lorelei. He didn't care about having a princess for a bride. As soon as he married her, Lorelei would be a princess anyway. So what was the difference?

He wouldn't even care that much about becoming a king someday, if Archduke Percy wasn't such a monster.

The wind howled in the forest beyond the moat. He looked out his window. Sheets of rain poured down. Wherever Lorelei had been today, she'd have to be home by now. He wished he could peek in her window and see her, warm and dry and fast asleep, in an embroidered nightgown.

⚓ ⚓ ⚓

Had she seen a light? Way up ahead? So much water was coming down, it was hard to keep her eyes open. "Achoo!"

Lightning flashed, and Lorelei saw a castle. Towers and battlements, dark against the yellow-gray sky.

Who lived there? A royal family? A troll family? Ogres? An evil magician? Maybe she should stay in the forest. "Achoo!" No. She had to go on. For Trudy's sake.

She hurried across the drawbridge. "Achoo!" It would be dry inside. She'd be out of the wind. If the owner was an ogre and he decided to eat her, she'd warm up while she roasted. And if he was a decent ogre, he might even let her take a bath before he cooked her.

She knocked on the thick oak doors. The Chief Royal Night Watchman opened them. A dripping muddy maiden stood there. Another princess? She didn't look like much. But he had his orders, and he let her into the great hall. "Wait here," he barked.

Nicholas had seen the small figure cross the drawbridge. Another one, he thought. His parents weren't going to like having to get up in the middle of the night for her. He grinned sourly. They'd be sorry they hadn't put in a test for coming in the daytime.

He met his parents on the circular stairway to the great hall where the maiden stood shivering and sneezing.

He couldn't believe it. It was Lorelei! What was she doing here?

"SHE KNOCKED ON THE THICK OAK DOORS.."

Lorelei watched them come down the stairs. They weren't ogres and trolls. One of them even looked familiar. It was that nice Prince Nicholas. Lorelei's heart lurched a little.

She curtsied deeply. She sneezed and wobbled and almost fell over.

They have kind faces, Lorelei thought, but they look annoyed. Except the prince. He looks glad to see me. She sent him a special smile. And then she sneezed.

"Who are you?" King Humphrey boomed. "Which one are you?"

"I am—achoo!—Lorelei. You see—achoo!—I got—"

"Another princess," Nicholas interrupted loudly. "There's always room for one more." He winked at Lorelei, hoping she'd see and go along. Hoping his parents wouldn't see. "Who knows?" he added. "She might be the one to pass the princess tests."

Lorelei saw the wink. He wanted her to pretend to be a princess? She could, if he wanted her to. But why?

She curtsied again. "I am Princess Lorelei. Achoo!"

121

Ten

"How did you get here?" Queen Hermione asked. "Where's your carriage?"

"Um . . . achoo! Um, I don't have a carriage. Um . . ." What could she say? "Um . . . I . . . I was bewitched." That was it! "Achoo! A fairy put a spell on our whole court. My father was turned into a blacksmith. I became a blacksmith's daughter. I was—achoo!—a baby when it happened."

Quick thinking, Nicholas thought. She was clever, too.

"Absurd! Ridiculous!" King Humphrey roared. "There hasn't been a case or example of a fairy spell in a hundred years. Not since Queen Rosella and King Harold's reign."

"Achoo!"

The lass is crazy, the queen thought.

"Suppose she is a true princess?" Prince Nicholas said. "She might be the only one of the eighty maidens here who is." He hoped Lorelei was paying attention. "If you don't give her the tests, you'll never know. You won't be able to abdicate, Father. I'll never marry. You'll never have grand—"

"Son or heir, you're right." The king put an arm around Nicholas' shoulder. "The boy is correct or accurate."

Lorelei listened between sneezes. Tests? Had they said that if she passed some tests, she could marry Nicholas? Really?

Queen Hermione shrugged. It couldn't do any harm. A true blacksmith's daughter would certainly fail the tests. She rang her bell for the Chief Royal Chambermaid.

"Achoo! Excuse me. My Lady-in-Waiting was with me when we got lost. Achoo! She's still under the spell. She thinks she keeps house for a blacksmith." Lorelei told them about Trudy.

She's so kind! Nicholas thought.

"And our black stallion got lost too. He looks like a mule."

The king called for a groom to ride to the village of Snettering-on-Snoakes to see if Trudy and Leonard had gotten home safely.

Lorelei went upstairs with the Chief Royal Chambermaid. Nicholas followed them. She'll pass one test anyway, he thought, looking at her muddy footprints. She has small feet. But what about the rest?

⚓ ⚓ ⚓

The tests began first thing in the morning.

Lorelei had slept well. Her sheets were satin. The blankets were velvet. The mattress was stuffed with swans' feathers. Just like home. When she woke up, she wasn't even sneezing anymore.

Someone had laid a gown out for her, and a Royal Chambermaid was there to dress her. The gown was pretty, with diamonds sewn into the skirt and pearls sewn into the bodice. But it wasn't embroidered, which was a shame. And look at that! "That's funny," she said out loud.

The Royal Chambermaid curtsied. "What's funny, your ladyship?"

"Well . . ." You'd think they'd get it right for a princess. "The skirt on the gown—I don't mean to criticize—but it's lighter than the bodice."

So Lorelei passed the first test.

Three princesses hadn't noticed. Seventy-seven maidens sat down to breakfast, which was a simple meal. Poached eggs, dry toast, and half a grapefruit—Lorelei's favorite food for breakfast, lunch, and dinner.

While they ate, King Humphrey welcomed them to the kingdom or monarchy of Biddle. Then he explained about the tests, but he didn't say what any of them were. "In closing," he concluded, "let the truest princess conquer or win."

After breakfast, the king and queen and Nicholas gave the princesses and Lorelei a tour of the castle. King Humphrey lectured about Biddle as they went. Nicholas stayed near Lorelei, wishing he could warn her about each test, but the princesses might hear.

When the tour was over, everyone returned to the royal banquet hall for lunch—the next round in the true-princess test (although the contestants didn't know it).

The queen rang her bell, and Royal Serving Maids entered the royal banquet hall.

A salad was placed in front of Lorelei. She picked up her fork.

Now why was a bit of uncooked noodle mixed in with the lettuce? Quietly, she pointed it out to a Royal Serving Maid. And passed the salad test. So that was it, Lorelei thought. You had to guess what was wrong with the food. Funny test.

Five maidens didn't find the noodle. They were escorted out immediately.

Seventy-one to go, Nicholas thought. He noticed that the crocodile princess was still in the running.

Lorelei found the toothpick under the flounder. It wasn't hard, now that she knew what to look for. Nicholas breathed a sigh of relief.

Only one princess didn't find the toothpick.

Lorelei fished the tiny marshmallow out of her ragout. Eight princesses didn't. One of them was dragged away, yelling, "It isn't fair! Mine melted!"

Nicholas thought he was going to die of worry before the meal ended.

Lorelei found the flake of tuna on the chocolate cake icing. Four princesses didn't. The meal was over. Lorelei and the crocodile princess and fifty-seven other princesses remained in the game.

Eleven

After lunch the measuring began in the queen's bedchamber.

Nicholas and the king weren't allowed to view this part of the test. They waited in the throne room. King Humphrey listened to petitions from his subjects while Nicholas paced up and down, chewing his nails.

In the bedchamber Royal Chambermaids with tape measures checked every inch of every princess. If a princess was too tall, she was out. If she was too short, she was out. If her ears were too big, they were out and she was out.

The measuring took the rest of the day. Lorelei worried about the size of her nose. It was her worst feature. She pulled in her nostrils. When she looked in the mirror, she always thought that made her nose seem a little smaller.

Her nose squeaked by. A hair bigger and she would have had it.

The measuring went on.

The waist of one of the princesses was too big by a sixty-fourth of an inch. Queen Hermione said she was sorry, but if she let this maiden slip by, she wouldn't know where to draw the line.

When the measuring was over, only ten princesses and Lorelei were left. The queen led them to the throne room.

The crocodile princess entered first. Nicholas bit his finger so hard it bled. She smiled at him. Her teeth looked pointy. Where was Lorelei? He held his breath.

Lorelei was the ninth to enter the room. Nicholas started breathing again. They looked at each other. This was scary.

The king gave bouquets to the princesses and congratulated or applauded them on getting so far.

Nicholas wanted to yell, It's another trick! It's a test!

Lorelei held her bouquet away from her to examine it. Some flowers made her sneeze and some made her eyes water. Roses were okay. Daffodils were okay too. Lilies made her sneeze. So did peonies. What was that? Parsley? That wasn't a flower. This was a test! She pulled out the parsley and sneezed.

The bouquet test fooled everyone except the crocodile princess and Lorelei. The best and the worst, Prince Nicholas thought. He was trembling.

Both of them passed the tapestry test. Lorelei spotted the missing thread from twenty feet away. Nicholas wished she could get extra credit.

King Humphrey announced that they would have a light supper and go to bed. The final test or examination, he lied, would be tomorrow, or the day after today.

Lorelei didn't have a moment to talk privately with Nicholas. She could tell he wanted her to be the one to pass the test, but she wanted to hear him say it. She also wanted him to give her a hint about the big test tomorrow.

He wanted to get near her, too. If he could whisper

to her for just one second, he could tell her about the pea. But at supper she sat at the other end of the table, next to the king. Nicholas heard him telling her about his collection of unicorn horns or tusks.

The crocodile princess sat between the king and queen. Nicholas hated the way she ate. She seemed to swallow her food without chewing. And she kept looking at him and licking her lips.

Nicholas excused himself from the table. He went out to the garden and picked up a few large rocks. Then he slipped back into the castle and headed for Lorelei's bedchamber. He'd put the rocks under the top mattress, where she'd be sure to feel them.

But he couldn't get in. The Chief Royal Guard stood in front of the door. Nicholas tried to send him on an errand, but the fellow said that the king had told him not to budge for anyone or any person.

So then Nicholas said he'd leave a note for Princess Lorelei. But the Chief Royal Guard said, "Begging your pardon, Your Highness, no notes. I have my orders."

Nicholas couldn't do anything. By this time tomorrow either he'd be engaged to Lorelei, or Percival would be the future King of Biddle. Or he'd be engaged to the crocodile princess!

Twelve

Nicholas couldn't sleep. One second he was full of
hope. She'd passed all the tests so far! The next
second he was in despair. Nobody could feel a pea
through all those mattresses. And the crocodile
princess had a better chance than Lorelei. After all,
the crocodile princess was a real princess, not a
blacksmith's daughter.

But it didn't matter. If Lorelei failed, he'd marry
her anyway. And his parents would have fits. And
Percival would get the throne. He tossed. He turned.
He finally slept, and he dreamed of being eaten by
crocodiles and drowned in peas.

⚓ ⚓ ⚓

When Lorelei entered her room, she wondered why
her bed had so many mattresses. Last night it had

"SHE WONDERED WHY HER BED
HAD SO MANY MATTRESSES."

been an ordinary bed. She shrugged. Maybe they wanted her to have an extra-good night's sleep before the big test.

She climbed the ladder and slipped under the sheets. The bed was the softest she'd ever been in. She stretched and wriggled her toes. Mmm. Lovely!

The prince was so nice! Even if he weren't a prince, even if he were a blacksmith, she'd love him. But he *was* a prince, and that was even better.

She rolled over. She couldn't get comfortable. The sheets felt all right. Satin. Satin was good. The blankets were velvet. Velvet was good.

She closed her eyes.

Something was wrong. Her nose itched and her back ached. She climbed down from the bed and looked at it.

It had to be the mattresses. Maybe there was a pigeon feather in one of them. But which one? There were so many.

She'd never fall asleep. She'd be up all night. Then she wouldn't be at her best for the big test tomorrow. Maybe she could stretch out in front of the fireplace.

She spread a blanket on the floor and laid another one on top of it. Then she got in between them and closed her eyes. The hours crawled by. The floor was hard, but you expected a floor to be uncomfortable. You didn't expect it from a bed piled with twenty mattresses.

Lorelei turned over on her stomach. No better. She rolled back. Could she, Lorelei, actually become a princess? She'd passed every test so far. If she married Prince Nicholas, she'd live in a castle. And so would her father. She giggled. Trudy would be a real lady-in-waiting.

Trudy! She sat up. She'd forgotten to find out if Trudy had gotten home safely. What kind of queen would she make if she couldn't remember her subjects?

She lay down again. She'd ask first thing in the morning. What could the test tomorrow be like? Would they ask her questions? She didn't know anything about being a princess. She didn't know much about being a blacksmith's daughter either.

What if they asked her about laws! About geography! About how to sit on a throne! Lorelei was awake all night.

In the morning the Chief Royal Chambermaid led the two maidens to the throne room. Lorelei's bones ached, and the skin under her gown was black and blue.

King Humphrey and Queen Hermione and Prince Nicholas were sitting on their thrones. All the courtiers and subjects had been cleared out for the big moment.

The first thing Lorelei wanted to do was to find out about Trudy. Then she'd take whatever test they wanted. She'd probably fail it. But at least she'd know about Trudy.

The other maiden looked so rested and . . . Lorelei hated to admit it, but the other one was beautiful. Maybe by now Nicholas wanted her to win.

"Good morning, princesses or damsels," the king boomed.

"Did you sleep—" the queen began.

"Did you find out—" Lorelei began.

The doors to the throne room burst open. A man rushed in carrying a child in his arms. Lorelei thought the little boy didn't look right.

King Humphrey stood. "What or why—"

"Sire! I am a poor woodcutter! My son is sick, and I have no money to pay a wisewoman to cure him. I have nowhere to turn, except to you."

"Oh dear," Lorelei said. She ran to the child. "Does your forehead pulse?"

The boy nodded.

"Oh dear. Does it hurt to—"

Nicholas interrupted. "If you were a princess here," he asked the crocodile princess, "what would you do?"

This is the test! Lorelei thought. Maybe the boy wasn't really sick. But he looked sick.

The crocodile princess said, "They should be forbidden to trouble you with their problems. This man and his son must be put to death. That will cure the boy." And she smiled her slow smile.

"What would you do, Princess Lorelei?" Nicholas asked.

What was she supposed to say? Did that horrible one give the right answer? But if you couldn't help people—if you had to *kill* them to make them leave you alone—then she, Lorelei, didn't want to be a princess.

But then she'd have to give Nicholas up.

Well, it didn't matter what the right answer was. Somebody was sick! "Oh dear. I used to get sick when I was a little—uh—princess. I still do sometimes." She turned to the queen. "Do you have any betony?" Lorelei was sure she was ruining everything, because the queen looked so upset. "I need the leaves of the chaste tree, too. If you don't have that, some bugloss will do. Where's the kitchen?"

Queen Hermione didn't know what to say. So she rang for the Chief Royal Serving Maid.

"Princess Lorelei would be kind to our subjects, Father," Nicholas said, while they waited for the serving maid. "Whether or not she can feel a pea under twenty mattresses." He dropped to his knees so hard, he thought he had broken a kneecap. "Ouch!"

"Oh dear," Lorelei said. A pea? What was he talking about?

"My darling princess." Nicholas took Lorelei's hand. "Will you marry me?"

"Oh dear. Yes, I'll marry you. We'll need hot water. Does your stomach ache?" she asked the boy.

He nodded.

"Did you sleep or rest well last night, Princess Lorelei?" the king asked. He had to know, even though everything had gotten confused or mixed up.

"No," Lorelei said. "I couldn't get comfortable. So I slept on the floor."

"The pea!" said the queen.

"The pea or bean," said the king.

"Darling!" said the prince.

Epilogue

Lorelei cured the woodcutter's son. King Humphrey and Queen Hermione gave their consent or permission to the marriage of Prince Nicholas and Princess Lorelei.

On their wedding day Nicholas wore a doublet embroidered with parsley, a shirt embroidered with tape measures, and hose embroidered with noodles. Lorelei's hood and veil were embroidered with tuna fish. Her bodice was embroidered with green peas, and her skirt and train were embroidered with tiny mattresses.

Trudy (who was perfectly safe, of course) was furious that she hadn't gotten rid of Lorelei. But when she moved into the castle, the other Royal Servants showed her the good side of serving a bunch of persnickety monarchs. She learned to agree with them over a dinner of cream of asparagus soup, venison crown roast, and twelve-layer mocha-raspberry cake.

When Sam returned from the earldom of Pildenue, he moved into the palace too. He never understood exactly how Lorelei had become a princess. And he couldn't for the life of him understand why everyone called him Lord Blacksmith. But he liked living in a palace and shoeing the king's wonderful horses.

So they all lived happily ever after.

The End.

Princess Sonora and the Long Sleep

To Sylvia, my real fairy godmother

—G.C.L.

One

What a hideous baby, the fairy Arabella thought. She said, "My gift to Sonora is beauty." She touched the baby's yellow squooshed-up face with her wand.

The baby began to change. Her scrawny arms and legs became plump, and her blotchy yellow skin turned pink. Her pointy head became round. Honey-colored ringlets appeared on her scalp.

Ouch! It hurt to have your body change shape and to grow hair on your head in ten seconds. Sonora wailed.

King Humphrey II of Biddle thought, Why did the fairy do that? As his first-born child—as his lovey dovey oodle boodle baby—she had been fine the way she was. But he bowed low to the fairy.

"Thank you, Arabella. What a wonderful gift." A person could get into a lot of trouble for failing to thank a fairy.

Queen Hermione II picked up the yowling baby and cuddled her. Then she curtsied deeply and thanked the fairy too, even though she wanted to wail along with her daughter. Sonora looks six months old, the queen thought. I wanted to watch her grow.

Gradually Sonora stopped crying, and her mother put her back into the gilded cradle. Time for the second fairy gift.

The fairy Allegra waved her wand over the baby. "I give Sonora the gift of a loving heart."

Something was happening again, Sonora realized. But this was better. This didn't hurt. She pictured the tall being and the soft being who fed her and held her and made noises to her. They were nice! She loved them! She said, "Goo," and blew a wet bubble.

Adorable! King Humphrey II thought.

Sweet! Queen Hermione II thought.

"My turn!" The fairy Adalissia stepped up to the cradle.

Adalissia gave Sonora gracefulness. Then the fairy Annadora gave her good health, and the fairy Antonetta made her the smartest human in the world.

Not much changed when Sonora got good health, since she was healthy already. And not much changed when she got gracefulness, because month-old babies don't have much opportunity to be graceful. But something did happen when Antonetta made her a smart person. Sonora listened more closely when the nice beings thanked the fairy. She noticed her own name and knew that she'd heard it before.

Aurora, the sixth fairy, was flustered. She had planned to make Sonora the smartest person in the world, but that miserable Antonetta had stolen her gift. Now what could she give the baby? She could make the child beautiful. But no, Arabella had already used that one. Adalissia had done gracefulness. What was left? They were all looking at her. They were laughing behind their sympathetic faces, glad they had been at the head of the line.

"Er . . ." Aurora waved her wand vaguely. Then she had it. It was so simple. It was much better than Antonetta's. She leaned over the cradle and touched

Sonora on the nose with her wand. "My gift is brilliance. Sonora is ten times as smart as any human in the world." There.

Sonora felt something happen again, a tickle and a little shake inside her head. Then—it was done. She closed her eyes to think, really think, for the first time. She listened to the noise the tall being was making. She remembered all the noises people had made with their mouths since she'd been born. Some of the noises sounded alike. Some of them always went together.

Now the soft being was making noises. They were words! The noises were words. She was thanking the fairy for her gift. She was hoping that Sonora (that's me! that's me!) would use her extraordinary intelligence well.

Sonora opened her eyes. The soft being was her mother. She was beautiful, with her big brown eyes and those lips that liked to smile at Sonora. Of course she loved her mother, since the fairy had just given her a loving heart. Sonora wondered why the fairy had done that. Didn't she think Sonora might be naturally loving?

The fairy Adrianna came forward to the cradle. "My gift—"

The door to the royal nursery flew open. Adrianna gasped. The other fairies gasped. King Humphrey II gasped. Queen Hermione II gasped.

Sonora heard the gasps, but she could see only the things right above her, such as the pink dragon-shaped balloon that hung over the cradle. She thought, Why couldn't these fairies have given me something useful, like the ability to sit up and see what's going on?

A new fairy came in. She looked like all the others. Tall, with rubbery-looking wings, surrounded by a flickering rainbow of lights. Smiling like the others had been till a second ago.

Queen Hermione II rushed to the newcomer. "Belladonna! We're honored." In her mind she shouted, Don't hurt my baby! Don't hurt Sonora!

The fairy looked around the room. "Pretty nursery," she cooed in an extra-sweet voice. "Cuddly stuffed unicorn. Handsome dollcastle." She looked in the cradle. "Beautiful baby."

She looks angry, Sonora thought. You didn't have

to be a genius to see that.

Belladonna continued. "You failed to invite me to the naming ceremony of your only child. I suppose you have a reason?"

"We didn't invite you because we thought you . . ." The king stopped. He had been about to say they thought she was dead, but he couldn't say that. "We . . . uh . . . thought you'd moved away. We're so glad you could come."

"Can I get you some refreshment?" the queen asked. "We have some deli—"

"I didn't move. Nobody thinks I moved." The fairy circled the cradle. "Some stupid people think I'm dead, but let me tell you, I'm very much alive."

"We have some delicious—"

"You can't buy me off with food. Maybe you figured the kid would get enough gifts from the seven of them." Belladonna waved her wand at the other fairies.

They drew back.

Belladonna went on. "You thought you'd economize—only buy seven gold plates, seven gold forks, seven gold . . ."

It's true, King Humphrey II thought unhappily. We do only have seven gold place settings, but because we thought she was dead. Not because we're stingy.

Queen Hermione II tried again. "There's plenty— "

"Maybe you thought I couldn't come up with a good gift. You thought I would run out of ideas, like Aurora here."

But I did think of a good gift, Aurora thought. How many people are ten times as smart as everybody else?

Belladonna roared, "You think I'm stupid like her? Is that what you think? Hump? Herm? Hmm?"

"Of course we don't think you're stupid," King Humphrey II said.

"I'll show you I can think of a new and special gift." She leaned over the cradle. "Kitchy coo."

Oh no, Sonora thought, wincing at the furious face. Somebody stop her! Do something!

Everyone was silent, frozen.

I have to do it, Sonora thought. I have to talk her out of whatever she's going to do. "Excuse . . ." Her voice was too low. She'd never said anything before. She swallowed and tried again. "Excuse—"

Belladonna didn't hear. "Annadora gave the baby good health, which she will keep until my gift takes place. So my gift to the ootsy tootsy baby"—she waved her wand—"is that she will prick herself with a spindle and die!"

Two

When? Sonora wondered. When will I prick myself? When I'm eighty? Or in the next five minutes?

"I can't stay," Belladonna cackled. "I must fly." She vanished.

Queen Hermione II snatched Sonora up and held her tight.

Tears ran down King Humphrey II's face in rivers. What good was it being king if fairies could do this to you?

"It won't happen," the queen shouted. "I won't let it. You're not going to prick yourself with anything, sweetheart, baby dove."

Sonora wondered if her mother could prevent it. Or did it have to happen? If it had to happen, it had to happen. She'd just enjoy everything until it did.

Sonora breathed deeply. Her mother smelled so good.

The fairy Adrianna coughed. "Nobody seems to remember that I haven't given Sonora my gift yet."

King Humphrey II threw himself down on his knees and clutched the fairy's skirts. Queen Hermione II put Sonora back in her cradle and threw herself down on her knees too.

"Please save our baby," the king pleaded.

"I can't reverse another fairy's gift," Adrianna said, freeing her skirts from the king's grasp. "That would cause a fairy war, and believe me, you don't want that. I thought of making Sonora artistic. What do you think?"

"Can't you do anything to save her?" the queen sobbed.

"Tutors will teach her to draw and play the harp," the king said.

Adrianna went to the cradle. "Let me think." It was mean of Belladonna to kill the kid because of her parents' mistake. "I can change Belladonna's wish a little. She has to prick herself. I can't do anything about that. . . . I know." She waved the wand over

"'I CAN'T REVERSE ANOTHER FAIRY'S GIFT,'
ADRIANNA SAID."

the cradle. "Sonora will prick herself, but she will not die. My gift is that she will sleep for a hundred years instead of dying. Oh, this is brilliant!" The fairy beamed at the king and queen. "At the end of a hundred years a highly eligible prince will wake her by kissing her. How's that?"

Hmm, Sonora thought. A hundred years . . . her parents would be dead by the time she woke up! She started crying and howling and bawling. And wishing the fairy Allegra hadn't given her a loving heart.

King Humphrey II picked her up. "Funny baby." He bounced her up and down. "She doesn't cry when the fairy says she's going to die. But when Adrianna saves her . . ." He bowed to the fairy. "Then she cries."

"We can go to the banquet hall now," the queen said.

Sonora fought to catch her breath. She had to explain. "Wait," she said finally. "Wisten!" Talking was hard without teeth. She tried again. "Listen!" There. She'd done it.

The king's jaw dropped, and he almost dropped Sonora too.

"If I sleep for a hundred years, Mother and Father—" She started crying again. "Mother and Father will die before I wake up."

"She can talk!" the queen said.

"And what if I have a dog or—"

"You can talk!" King Humphrey II lifted Sonora way above his head. "The ibble bibble baby can talk!"

And Belladonna said I couldn't think of a good gift, the fairy Aurora thought, smirking. How many gifts make month-old babies talk?

"Don't let them die while I'm asleep," Sonora begged.

She's right, the queen thought. But we can't criticize Adrianna's gift. She could get mad and harm Sonora.

"Um . . ." Adrianna said. If she really wanted to help Sonora, she had to fix as much as she could. "Suppose I do it this way. Suppose, when Sonora falls asleep, everybody in the castle sleeps along with her."

"Excellent," the king said. "Except sometimes we're in the courtyard."

"All right." She waved her wand. "Everybody from

161

the moat on in will fall asleep and sleep for a hundred years." She chuckled. "Sweet dreams."

⚓ ⚓ ⚓

When the fairies left, King Humphrey II and Queen Hermione II had a long talk about the hundred-year sleep. They should have included Sonora, who would have had lots of good ideas. But Sonora was in the nursery, being rocked in her cradle by a Royal Nursemaid.

"Maybe it doesn't have to happen," the queen said, brushing away a tear. "We'll be very groggy when we wake up."

"We'll issue a proclamation," King Humphrey II said. "No spindles inside the castle."

"No needles," Queen Hermione II added. "Nothing sharp. Maybe if *anything* pricks her she'll fall asleep."

"No knives. No swords. No toothpicks. We'll build a shed and keep everything in there."

"Belladonna didn't say when Sonora would prick herself," the queen said. "She could be fifty when she does it."

"No prince will marry her if he knows she's going to nap for a hundred years," the king said. "He could be out hunting, and when he comes home, nobody greets him. They're all fast asleep."

The queen agreed. "Besides, the servants would panic if they knew. The whole court would leave."

They decided to keep the hundred-year sleep a secret. They didn't think of telling Sonora to keep it a secret too, because they kept forgetting how smart she was. But they didn't need to tell her because she already knew. She'd figured it out ten seconds after Adrianna gave the gift. Now, while she lay in the darkened nursery, she was thinking it all over instead of sleeping. She'd save sleeping for her hundred-year snooze.

The fairy's gift would come true, Sonora decided. If her head could change shape and if she could become plump just because of a fairy, not to mention getting smart twice, then of course she'd prick herself and sleep for a hundred years.

Sonora also figured out that her parents would try to keep the gift from happening by hiding the spindles. But wherever they were hidden, she'd find them and take one. She wasn't going to prick herself by accident at the worst possible moment. No. She would do it on purpose when the time was exactly right.

Three

The Royal Nursemaids couldn't get used to Sonora. It was so strange to change the diaper of a baby who was reading a book, especially a baby who blushed and said, "I'm so sorry to bother you with my elimination."

In her bath, Sonora never played with her cute balsa mermaids and whales. Instead, she'd remind the Royal Nursemaids to wash behind her ears and between her toes. After the bath, she'd refuse to wear her adorable nightcap with the floppy donkey ears. She'd say it wasn't dignified.

The king and queen had trouble getting used to Sonora too. The king hated to watch her eat. It was unnatural to see a baby in a high chair manage a spoon and fork so perfectly. She never dribbled a drop on her yellow linen bib with the pink bunny rabbits scampering across it.

There were hundreds of things that the queen missed. Sonora never tried to fit her foot into her mouth. After her second word, "wisten," she never said another word of baby talk. She never drooled. She never gurgled. She refused to breastfeed. She admitted that it was good for her, but she said it was a barbaric, cannibalistic custom. Queen Hermione II wasn't certain what a cannibal was, but she was embarrassed to ask a little baby, even though she knew Sonora would be perfectly polite about it. Even though she knew Sonora would be delighted to be asked.

But then again, in some ways Sonora was exactly like other babies. She had to be burped like anybody else, although other babies didn't go on and on about how silly they felt waiting for the burp to come. And most babies didn't cry from shame when they spit up on someone.

Because of her loving heart, Sonora also cried whenever anybody stopped holding her. Queen Hermione II could explain that her lap was falling asleep from holding Sonora and the heavy volume on troll psychology Sonora was reading. It didn't matter. She cried anyway. It didn't matter either if King Humphrey II said he had to meet with his Royal Councillors. Sonora cried anyway. And when the king said she was too young to help decide matters of state, her loving heart and her brilliant mind were in complete agreement—she had a temper tantrum.

She learned to crawl at about the same time as other babies, although she was more of a perfectionist about it than most. She set daily distance goals for herself, and she only crawled in perfectly straight lines and perfectly round circles. After a day of crawling practice, she once told her father that she enjoyed watching "the miracle of child development" happening to her.

Although her overall health was excellent, sometimes she got sick just like other children. Except other children didn't diagnose their own diseases or tell the Chief Royal Physician what the treatment should be. And other children got well faster than Sonora, because other children listened when their parents told them to go to sleep. Sonora wouldn't listen and wouldn't sleep.

Most nights, sick or well, she'd crawl into the royal library. She could memorize five or six books in a typical night. Fairy tales were her favorites. The more she knew about fairies, she reasoned, the better off she'd be.

On nights when she didn't feel like reading, she'd lie in her crib and think up questions. Then she'd answer them. For example, why did bread rise? She knew about yeast, but yeast wasn't the whole answer—because why did yeast do what it did? The whole answer fit in with Sonora's Law of the Purposeful Behavior of Everything Everywhere. Bread's purpose, she knew, was to feed people. It rose so it could feed as many people as possible. The reason jumped out at you when you thought about it correctly.

She decided that when her hand was big enough to hold a pen comfortably, she'd write a monograph on the subject.

Sonora didn't learn everything by reading and thinking. She also learned from the people around her. As soon as she could walk, she followed the Royal Dairymaids everywhere and asked them a

"SHE FOLLOWED THE ROYAL DAIRYMAIDS
EVERYWHERE AND ASKED THEM A MILLION
QUESTIONS."

million questions about milking. She watched the Chief Royal Blacksmith and asked him questions. She spent days in the kitchen with the Chief Royal Cook, until the Chief Royal Cook wanted to pound Sonora on her Royal Head with the Royal Frying Pan.

Once she found out everything the Royal Dairymaids knew about milking or the Chief Royal Blacksmith knew about smithing or the Chief Royal Cook knew about cooking, Sonora would get to work. She'd read every book there was on the subject. Then she'd think, and soon she'd come up with a better or faster way to milk or smith or cook or do anything else.

She'd be very excited. If it was the middle of the night, she wouldn't be able to wait until morning to talk about her discovery, so she'd wake her parents up. This was always a disappointment. The king and queen were too sleepy to listen, and sometimes they were grumpy about being awakened. The king even raised his voice once, when she woke him to say she'd found a way to grow skinless potatoes, which would save hours of peeling.

Sonora would imagine the joy her improvements would bring the Chief Royal Farmer or the Chief Royal Cook or the Royal Dairymaids. But she'd be wrong—they were hardly ever pleased. They liked doing things the way they were used to, and they didn't like being told how to do their business by a Royal Pipsqueak no bigger than a mosquito bite.

Sonora couldn't understand it. She knew that the purpose of dairymaids was more than to milk cows. They were people, and people had lots of purposes. If her brain hadn't told her that, her loving heart would have. But part of their purpose was to get milk from cows, so she couldn't understand why they didn't want to do it in the best way possible.

In fact, nobody was nearly as interested in what Sonora knew as she wanted them to be. Even her mother wasn't. Often, while the queen wrote out menu plans, Sonora would talk about her latest research.

And for the thousandth time the queen would wish that Aurora had thought of a different gift. A simple one would have been fine, Queen Hermione II would think. An excellent sense of smell would have been good, or a pretty singing voice, which didn't run in the family. She and Humphrey II both sounded like frogs.

Then the queen would try not to yawn. What was the child telling her now? How to build the fastest sailboat in the world? But Biddle was landlocked, and even its lakes were small. A *slow* sailboat could cross the biggest one pretty quickly. Queen Hermione II's eyes would close then, and her handwriting on the menu would wobble.

And Sonora would feel terrible, even though she'd know her mother didn't mean to hurt her feelings.

It would be the same with the king. He'd be deciding which squires were ready to be knighted, for example. Meanwhile, she'd start telling him about a book she'd read, a book that had been in his library forever without his ever wanting to read a word of it.

He'd say, "Sonora, sweet, we're not as smart as you are. We can't think about knights and dwindling— um, dwindling what? What's dwindling, cutie pie?"

"Dwindling unicorn habitats."

"That's right, darling. Tell us about it later when we're not so busy."

Sonora would leave then, knowing that her father

171

hoped she'd never mention a unicorn to him again—
with or without a dwindling habitat.

A new proverb sprang up in Biddle. Whenever a
Biddler asked a question that nobody could answer,
someone would say, "Princess Sonora knows." Then
somebody else would say, "But don't ask her."

And everybody would laugh.

Four

When Sonora was six, she read every book she could find on the art of picking locks. Then, on a dark night, she stole out of the castle and went to the shed that held the spindles and the other sharp things. The moment had come for her to get her very own spindle so she'd be able to prick herself when the time was right.

She set to work, ignoring the sign on the door that said, "Keep out! Do not enter! Private property! Danger! Get out of here!" It took her exactly twelve minutes to pick all ten locks and another fifteen minutes to very carefully remove the spindle from the first spinning wheel she came to. When that was done, she picked the spindle up with the tongs from the nursery fireplace and carried it very carefully back to the nursery, where she dropped it in the bottom of her toy chest. She left it there, under the toys her parents had gotten for the child they expected to have—the one who wasn't ten times as smart as anybody else.

⚓ ⚓ ⚓

Every year King Humphrey II and Queen Hermione II made a birthday party for Sonora, which never turned out well. The party for Sonora's tenth birthday began like all the rest. The lads and lasses had come only because they had to. They stood around in the tournament field, feeling silly in their party caps. Sonora tried to be a good hostess and make them feel comfortable, but every subject she brought up fell flat. Nobody wanted to discuss whether fairies and elves should obey Biddle's laws, or who was happier, all things being equal, the knight or his horse.

Nobody wanted to play any games either. They had played hide-and-seek last year, and Sonora had told them how to play it better. It had taken months to forget her advice and get their good old game back.

The year before that she had ruined blindman's buff.

They all sighed, including Sonora. It would be hours before she could return to her latest project, finding out why things had colors.

Then she had an inspiration. She called for ink, quill pens, and parchment for everyone. When the supplies came, she began to interview each guest in turn. Sonora listened and took notes while everybody who wasn't being interviewed grumbled about how stupid and boring this was.

When the last guest had been interviewed, Sonora cleared her throat nervously. This was the first time she had spoken before an assembly. She said, "Silence." Gradually everybody got quiet. "From my notes, I see that none of you enjoys doing chores."

The lads and lasses groaned. Now the know-it-all was going to tell them how to be better children.

"Here are seven good ways to avoid doing them."

The lads and lasses began to write as fast as they could. During the rest of that wonderful party, which flew by much too quickly for everybody, Sonora told them how to stay out late to play, how to get even with their enemies and not get caught, how not to eat food they didn't like, and how not to go to bed at bedtime (Sonora's specialty).

When the party was over, Sonora told the guests to bring their homework next year and she'd do it for them. As they left, everyone told the king and queen that it had been the best party ever. King Humphrey II and Queen Hermione II were delighted. They told Sonora she'd be a popular queen someday.

But Sonora knew better. When the lads and lasses grew up to be Royal Bakers or Royal Chimney Sweeps, they'd dislike her advice as much as their parents did. And they'd laugh and say the proverb to each other. "Princess Sonora knows, but don't ask her."

The evening after the party, Sonora moved out of the nursery to her own grown-up bedchamber, which had only one thing wrong with it—a bed. Sonora had argued that she didn't need a bed and didn't want a bed and disliked beds very much. It didn't matter, though. She was stuck with it.

Late that night, when everybody else was asleep, she used her new fireplace tongs to carry the spindle very carefully from the toy chest in the nursery to the floor of her new wardrobe. She shoved it all the way to the back and covered it with a pile of the nightdresses she refused to wear.

Then she tried to forget about the spindle and a hundred years of sleep.

☙ ☙ ☙

The right time for Sonora to prick herself didn't come. And the more time passed, the less she wanted to do it. She was only a little frightened by the hundred years. What she was most afraid of was sleep.

She hadn't slept at all since the fairy Aurora made her so smart. She'd seen her mother sleep, usually when Sonora was trying to explain something. She'd seen her father fall asleep while listening to the Royal Minstrels after dinner. Sometimes Sonora yawned when they sang, but then she'd sit up extra straight and open her eyes extra wide. She'd stay awake because sleeping people were scary. They were right in the room with you, sort of. Their bodies were, but their minds weren't, which was creepy. Sonora loved her mind, and she wanted to know where it was at all times.

When Sonora was fourteen, King Humphrey II and Queen Hermione II decided on a husband for her, if she didn't prick herself before the wedding. They chose Prince Melvin XX, heir apparent to the throne of the neighboring kingdom of Kulornia. He was the ideal choice. Kulornia was even bigger and richer than Biddle. Sonora would be queen over a vast empire.

King Humphrey II sent a dispatch to King Stanley CXLIV, the prince's father. He also sent a portrait of Sonora. King Stanley CXLIV sent back his answer.

King Humphrey II opened the dispatch and read it. "King Stanley CXLIV has agreed to the wedding," he told Sonora and Queen Hermione II. "The prince is coming for a visit." A piece of foolscap fell to the marble floor of the throne room. King Humphrey II picked it up. "Oh, look. Here's a letter from the prince." He started reading.

My dear Princess,
My father, King Stanley CXLIV, says I'm going to marry you. I believe him. He always tells

the truth, so I believe him. If he were a liar, I wouldn't.

King Humphrey II nodded. "He sounds sensible."
He sounds like a fool, Sonora thought.
The king went on reading.

I believe in honesty. The fairies made me Honest when I was born. Besides, I do what my father tells me. If he says to marry someone, I marry her. I'm Traditional. The fairies made me that too when I was born. Below is a list of all the other things they made me.

1. *Brave.*
2. *Handsome.*
3. *Strong.*
4. *A Man of Action. (I used to be a Baby of Action.)*
5. *A Good Dancer.*
6. *Tall.*

Plus Honest and Traditional, as shown above. I trust you will find me as described.

> *Honestly,*
> *Prince Melvin XX*

"Sweetheart!" Queen Hermione II said. "He's just right for you. He's handsome and you're beautiful. He's a good dancer and you're graceful." They would have so much to share. The queen felt weepy. Her baby was leaving her.

Sonora also felt weepy. They had nothing in common. Nothing important. The fairies hadn't made him smart. They hadn't given him a loving heart. Was it time to get out the spindle and prick herself?

Five

In her room, Sonora reached into her wardrobe. She touched the nightdresses that covered the spindle. Her heart raced. The moment had come.

But she didn't want to go to sleep.

Maybe the moment hadn't come. Maybe Prince Melvin XX wasn't so bad. His letter was so bad. But maybe he wasn't. Maybe he was just not a talented writer. He probably wasn't brilliant, but that might not matter. At least people wouldn't make up horrible proverbs about not asking him the things he knew. Besides, maybe he was really wonderful.

He couldn't be.

Maybe he was. If she went to sleep now, she'd never find out. He'd get old and die before she woke up. And she'd have missed the great romance of her life.

It wouldn't hurt to find out. He was coming soon. She could always prick herself after she met him.

⚓ ⚓ ⚓

Prince Melvin XX came, following forty pages blowing trumpets. Sonora met him in the courtyard as he stepped down from his carriage. Probably he was handsome, but he was so tall she could hardly see his face, because it was too far away. He had dark hair and broad shoulders. She couldn't tell what color his eyes were. She'd have to wait to see them when he sat down.

She curtsied.

He bowed. He thought, I guess she's pretty. She's puny though. The fairies didn't make her Tall.

They had no chance to talk because they had to hurry to a banquet in the prince's honor. Sonora sat at one end of the banquet table with her mother. Prince Melvin XX sat with her father at the other end.

The prince ate, chewing very slowly. Sonora watched his mouth. He ate more slowly than anyone she had ever seen before. While he ate, he talked to the king. The prince spoke so slowly that King Humphrey II forgot the beginning of each sentence by the time Prince Melvin XX got to the end. Prince Melvin XX told the king about every second of his journey to Biddle. He explained how he had decided on each item he had brought from Kulornia. He said what he had been doing when his father had agreed to the marriage.

King Humphrey II wished there weren't so many courses. Another half hour of this and he'd faint.

The meal finally ended. King Humphrey II stood up quickly. "Sonora, sweet, show your guest the garden." Get him out of here!

Sonora curtsied and led the prince away. Queen Hermione II headed for her daughter's bedchamber to see what Sonora needed for her trousseau. The king decided to take a nap.

⚓ ⚓ ⚓

Prince Melvin XX held the door to the garden open for Sonora. "My father says you're smart," he said slowly. "And I believe him. He always tells the truth. If he were a liar, I wouldn't believe him."

"That's reasonable." Sonora tried to smile, but she

couldn't. I can't smile because I'm sad, she thought. If I were happy, I would be able to. Aaa! I'm thinking the way he talks. "Our roses are over here."

"I see them. The red ones are very red." He went on. "I'm glad you're smart. When I'm king, you can write my proclamations. I'll tell you what to say."

"If you tell me what to say, why—"

"Thinking gets in the way. People can be too smart. I'm a Man of Action. The fairies made me that way. I always know what to do. Father had to write a proclamation the other day . . ."

Sonora bent over to sniff a peony. Here was another person who would never want to listen to her.

⚓ ⚓ ⚓

The king couldn't fall asleep. His head hurt too much. Compared to the prince, Sonora was a pleasure to listen to. He rolled over onto his stomach.

⚓ ⚓ ⚓

In Sonora's room, Queen Hermione II began to take gowns out of the wardrobe and spread them across Sonora's bed. The child needed new ones for her trousseau. Five or ten new gowns. The prettiest gown Sonora had was blue, embroidered with seed pearls. Where was it? She turned back to the wardrobe.

⚓ ⚓ ⚓

Sonora and Prince Melvin XX stood next to the weeping cherry tree. He was talking as usual. She had stopped listening an hour ago. He was saying very slowly that he didn't see much use for flowers. Vegetables were different. He saw a use for them. He began to list all the vegetables he could think of.

Sonora wondered how bad sleep could be. A hundred years of sleep would be shorter than five minutes with the prince. As soon as she got away from him, she'd go to her room and prick herself.

No! If she did, he'd fall asleep too, and in a hundred years she'd still have to marry him. But then she wouldn't have a hundred years of sleep to look forward to. So she couldn't prick herself now. She'd have to wait and do it when he went back to Kulornia to get ready for the wedding.

"I especially like boiled corn in the . . ."

But meanwhile she didn't have to spend hours with him. She could think of an excuse to get away. She wasn't so smart for nothing.

"Do you like corn too?"

He'd stopped talking. He was looking at her, waiting. He must have asked her something.

"I'm sorry. What did you say?"

"I said do you like corn too?" Was she hard of hearing? That wouldn't be good. His own hearing was perfect.

"Not particularly." Maybe he wouldn't want to marry her if she didn't like corn.

"Oh." He shrugged. "I never met anybody who didn't like it before."

"Sir, I fear I must leave you for a while. The king likes me to use this hour for quiet meditation in my room. I will—"

"Corn might be my favorite—"

She fled.

⚓ ⚓ ⚓

The queen lifted the last gown off its hook. Where was the blue one? Was that it on the floor of the wardrobe? She bent down to see. But it wasn't the gown. It was a pile of old nightdresses. How could the Royal Chambermaids have left them in such a heap? They could have been there for years. Queen Hermione II started pulling them out. She'd fold them up and shame the wenches with them.

Something underneath. What—

"Aaaaa! Aaaaa! Aaaaa! Help! Treason! Aaaaa! Aaaaa!" Have to get it out of here! "Aaaaa!" Protect Sonora! "Aaaaa!" She grabbed the spindle. "Aaaaa!" Had to run! She ran around the room, not knowing where to go. "Aaaaa!" The shed! She had to get it to the shed! "Aaaaa!" She ran out of the room.

Sonora heard her mother's screams and thought, Spiders! She started running. Tarantulas! The screams sounded like they were coming from her own room. She thought, Black widows! I warned Father just last week. I have to reach Mother! I'm the only one who knows what to do if she's bitten.

The king sat up in bed. Was someone yelling?

The prince lifted his head. Someone was screaming. Was there a dragon? He looked up at the sky. He didn't see a dragon, so one couldn't be there.

"Aaaaa!" The queen raced down the north corridor, away from Sonora's room.

"'AAAA!' THE QUEEN TURNED THE CORNER.
"'COMING! DON'T WOR—' SONORA TURNED
THE CORNER."

Sonora raced up the west corridor, toward her room.
Let me reach her in time!

"Aaaaa!" The queen turned the corner.

"Coming! Don't wor—" Sonora turned the corner.

The spindle pierced Sonora's outstretched hand.

Six

In the meadow across the moat, Elbert watched his father's flock of sheep. It was a boring job. The only time it was interesting was when the castle drawbridge was lowered. Then Elbert could watch who was going in and coming out, and he could also see into the castle courtyard.

The drawbridge was lowered now. A team of oxen was crossing with a wagonload of peaches. Juicy, ripe peaches. Elbert's mouth watered. Inside the courtyard, a butcher was cutting up a spring lamb. Elbert's stomach rumbled. He could almost taste it—roast lamb followed by peach pie.

On the drawbridge, the oxen stopped, and the driver slumped forward.

Huh? Elbert stared.

The driver almost fell off his bench. The heads of the oxen drooped. In the courtyard, the butcher stopped cutting. His head lolled to one side.

Arrows! Had to be arrows! Elbert spun around. No arrows were flying. He spun back. No arrows were sticking out of the wagon driver. None stuck out of the oxen.

He jumped up. Maybe he could help! Maybe he could get a few peaches and that lamb.

What was that? Something was growing along the outer rim of the moat. He started running. Whatever it was, it was growing fast—as high as his knee already. But he didn't have far to go. He ran faster. The hedge was as high as his waist. He'd jump over, grab the wagon driver, and drag him to safety.

He reached the moat. But the hedge was now up to his neck. He could still climb it, but he'd never get the driver out, and he'd get caught inside too. He stood before the hedge, panting. In his last glimpse of the drawbridge, Elbert saw one of the oxen switch its tail to brush away a fly. The ox was alive! It was—it was—asleep!

The hedge zoomed up, taller than Elbert. Taller

than twice his height. Tall as the old maple in front of his cottage. Tall as the church steeple.

Elbert turned back to his sheep. Now herding was going to be completely boring, without the drawbridge and courtyard to watch.

⚓ ⚓ ⚓

The queen's last wide-awake thought was: The child will spend the next hundred years lying on a cold stone floor.

The king's last thoughts were: Our headache's gone. We feel sleepy. We could sleep for a hundred years.

The prince's last thought was: I could take a nap. Sleep is good for you. My father told me that . . .

Sonora's last thought was: Oh no, I'll have to marry him. Aaaaa!

⚓ ⚓ ⚓

The fairy Adrianna appeared in the courtyard. The hedge looked good. It was high and dense and prickly, with thorns as long as her wand.

In the castle she stood over the sleeping forms of Sonora and Queen Hermione II. I can't leave them on the floor, she thought. She waved her wand, and the queen floated to the bed in the royal bedchamber, next to the king. Then she moved Sonora to her room and arranged her gracefully on the bed. She placed a wooden sign on Sonora's stomach. In flowing script it said, *"I am Princess Sonora. Kiss me, prince, and I shall be yours forever."*

Sonora wouldn't have liked that, not one little bit.

Prince Melvin XX was sneezing in his sleep, stretched out in a bed of clover. The fairy moved him to a wooden bench. Then she left without making anybody else more comfortable. They weren't royal, and they could make the best of wherever they happened to be.

In the next hour she appeared here and there throughout Biddle. She told everyone she saw that the royal family had gone on a journey. She said she had created the hedge to keep things safe while they were away.

Everyone believed her—everyone except Elbert the shepherd.

That night Elbert started building a very tall ladder, the tallest one in Biddle. A week later, when the ladder was finished, he dragged it to the hedge and climbed up.

The peaches were brown and rotten. The dead lamb was covered with flies. But everything else was the same. The oxen stood on the drawbridge, their heads drooping. The butcher leaned over his chopping block, the knife still in his hand. While Elbert watched, the butcher lazily reached up with his other hand to scratch his nose. They were all still asleep!

But why? Elbert wondered. Princess Sonora knows, he thought, but don't ask her. He laughed. Don't ask her because she's sleeping.

Seven

Sonora dreamed it was her wedding day. The great hall was filled with guests. Prince Melvin XX stood next to her. The Chief Royal Councillor was reciting the wedding ceremony. The prince hadn't moved once the whole time. He's like a block of wood, Sonora thought.

The ceremony was almost over. The Chief Royal Councillor said, "Prince Melvin XX, will you say a few words?"

The prince began to speak. Sonora saw a hinge at the corner of his mouth. She looked at his arm next to her. It was carved of wood! He was a big wooden puppet.

"Weddings are good. Everybody has fun at a wedding. There's always . . ."

Everyone clapped. Prince Melvin XX kept right on

talking. Sonora screamed, "Aaaaaaaaaaaaaaaaa-aaaaa . . ."

⚓ ⚓ ⚓

When Prince Melvin XX didn't return to Kulornia, King Stanley CXLIV sent a messenger to Biddle. The messenger came back and told the king about the journey the royal family was thought to have made. King Stanley CXLIV reasoned that the prince must have left with them. He wondered where they'd gone and hoped it was a good place for an Honest, Traditional, Brave, Handsome, Strong, and Tall Man of Action who was also a Good Dancer.

Five years passed. King Stanley CXLIV died, and Prince Melvin XX's younger brother, Prince Roger XCII, was crowned king of Kulornia. His first act as king was to annex the kingdom of Biddle, the kingdom without a king.

The saying "Princess Sonora knows, but don't ask her" spread from Biddle to Kulornia.

⚓ ⚓ ⚓

Queen Hermione II dreamed that Sonora was a little girl again. She was in the queen's lap, talking about the hissing turtle. Sonora said that the turtle hisses to fool people into thinking it's a whistling teakettle. Then why does the teakettle whistle? the queen asked. Because it doesn't know how to sing, Sonora explained. And Queen Hermione II thought, She's an extraordinary child.

⚓ ⚓ ⚓

Ten years passed. The shepherd Elbert's son Elmo was four years old. Elbert dragged his long ladder to the hedge again. He climbed the ladder with Elmo in his arms. "See," he whispered into his son's ear. "They're all asleep. Fast asleep."

⚓ ⚓ ⚓

King Humphrey II dreamed that he was writing a proclamation making the beaver the Royal Rodent of Biddle. He wrote each word as clearly as he could. But as soon as he finished a word and went on to the next, the letters in the last word changed. For instance, "beaver" changed to

"HE CLIMBED THE LADDER WITH ELMO IN
HIS ARMS."

"molar," and "rodent" changed to "jerkin." It was very annoying.

⚓ ⚓ ⚓

Every few years, Elbert's sons and grandsons and great-grandsons climbed the ladder to look at the sleeping court of Biddle.

⚓ ⚓ ⚓

Fifty years passed. Prince Melvin XX's grand-nephew, Prince Simon LXIX, heir apparent to the throne of Greater Kulornia, had a son. Prince Simon LXIX's wife, Bernardine LXI, the princess apparent, invited the fairies to her son Jasper CCX's naming ceremony. She invited all eight of them, including Belladonna, so no one would have hurt feelings.

There was trouble anyway. The fairies started argu-ing over who was the most powerful. Adrianna bel-lowed that she was the most powerful and she could prove it. So she turned the princess apparent into a shoehorn. Not to be outdone, Allegra changed the princess from a shoehorn into a baby troll. Then

Antonetta turned her into a lady's wig. In the space of a half hour, poor Bernardine LXI became a piccolo, a crab apple tree, a quill pen, and a green peppercorn.

In the end they turned her back into a princess. But no one was certain if they had turned her into the same princess she was before. She was a little different from then on, maybe because one of the fairies had made an eensy teensy mistake, or maybe because the experience had been so terrifying.

Whatever the reason, when the princess apparent gave birth to a daughter two years later, no fairies were invited to the new baby's naming ceremony. Prince Simon LXIX worried about fairy revenge, but there was none. Each fairy blamed another fairy for the ban, so they didn't get mad at the prince, but they didn't give the child any gifts either.

And that was the end of the custom of having fairies at naming ceremonies.

⚓ ⚓ ⚓

Prince Melvin XX dreamed about armor. He was polishing all the parts of his armor. While he polished, he named each piece. "One polished helmet. One polished visor. One polished haute-piece. One polished pauldron." And so on.

‎⚓ ⚓ ⚓

Eighty-three years later, Prince Melvin XX's great-grandnephew, King Jasper CCX, had a son, Prince Christopher I, or plain Prince Christopher.

Even though the fairies didn't give him any gifts, Christopher had a loving heart. He was smart, but not ten times as smart as everybody else. And he was handsome, pretty handsome anyway. But mostly he was curious. When he started talking, his first word was "why." And most of his sentences from then on started with "Why."

Why is your nose above your lips and not somewhere else?

Why are diapers white?

Why do you have nails on your fingers and toes? Why don't you have them anywhere else?

Why are peas round?

Why do birds have so many feathers?

He'd ask anybody anytime. The noble children of

Kulornia liked Christopher, but they hated playing with him. If they were playing ice hockey, for example, he'd stop the game to ask why ice is harder to see through than water. If they were racing, he'd halt right before the finish line and ask why grass doesn't have leaves. Once, Christopher and his best friend, the young Duke Thomas, were watching a tournament. Just as the two champion knights galloped at each other, Christopher nudged his friend and pointed at a flock of geese flying above the stadium. "Look." Thomas did while Christopher whispered, "Why don't they flap their tail feathers too?" By the time Thomas looked down again, one knight was lying in the dirt and the other was trotting out of the arena.

Occasionally Thomas could answer one of Christopher's questions, but not often. Christopher's page could answer a few more questions, but then he'd be stumped. Christopher's tutors could answer even more, but then they'd be stumped. His parents could answer yet more, but they'd finally be stumped too.

When they were stumped, they all said the same thing. They all said, "Princess Sonora knows, but don't ask her." And when he asked who Princess Sonora was, they all told him it was just an expression. There was no such person.

It was the answer he hated most in the whole wide world.

Eight

As Prince Christopher grew older, he tried to answer his own questions. He read as much as he could in King Jasper CCX's library. He found some answers, but not enough, never enough.

Whenever his research got interesting, something always took him away from it. He'd have to practice his jousting. Or he'd have to try on a new suit of armor, or attend a banquet, where his father would forbid him to ask the guests even one single measly question.

A week after Christopher's seventeenth birthday, he was in the library, trying to find out if a dragon ever burns the roof of its mouth. A stack of books was piled next to him. He picked up the top one, *Where There's Dragon, There's Fire*. One of the chapters was about dragon skin. Did skin or something else cover the inside of a dragon's mouth? He opened to page 3,832.

A Royal Squire came into the library. "Majesty, the king wants you to come to the audience room."

Christopher slammed the book shut. It never failed.

Ten shepherds and one sheep faced the king in the audience room. As soon as Christopher took his place next to King Jasper CCX, the oldest shepherd began to speak.

"Highness, something terrible is happening to our sheep. See?" He pointed to the sheep. "She's going bald. They all are. In the spring, there won't be much fleece for us to sell."

Christopher saw big bald spots on the sheep's back.

Another shepherd said, "In the winter, they'll catch cold. It's only October, and they're already starting to sneeze."

The sheep sneezed.

King Jasper CCX said, "God bless you." Then he called for his Chief Royal Veterinarian.

The Chief Royal Veterinarian spread a smelly ointment all over the sheep's bald spots. Then she gave

"THE CHIEF ROYAL VETERINARIAN SPREAD A SMELLY
OINTMENT ALL OVER THE SHEEP'S BALD SPOTS."

the shepherds a vat of the ointment to spread on all the sheep.

A week later the shepherds and the sheep were back in the audience room. The bald spots were bigger. The sheep sneezed twice.

The Chief Royal Veterinarian told the shepherds to keep putting the ointment on the sheep. She also gave them medicine for the sheep to drink.

Two weeks later the shepherds and the sheep were back. Now the sheep had no wool left, and she never stopped sneezing.

The Chief Royal Veterinarian shook her head. "I don't know the cure," she said. "Princess Sonora knows, but don't ask her."

King Jasper CCX asked Prince Christopher what he thought.

As usual, the prince had a question. "Could we send for all the shepherds in Greater Kulornia? Maybe one of them knows how to cure the balding disease."

It was done. Shepherds came from all over Kulornia and also from the land that used to be Biddle. Four hundred shepherds camped outside Kulornia castle. One of them was Elroy, Elbert's great-great-grandson.

King Jasper CCX talked to half of the shepherds, and Prince Christopher talked to the other half. The first one hundred and ninety-nine shepherds Christopher talked to said their sheep weren't getting bald and they didn't know how to cure the balding disease.

The last shepherd Christopher spoke to was Elroy.

"Are your sheep going bald?" the prince asked.

"No, your majesty."

"Do you know how to cure the balding disease?"

"I'm sorry, but I don't, your highness. Princess Sonora knows, but don't ask her . . ."

Christopher turned away.

". . . because she's asleep."

Christopher spun around. *"What? What do you mean, she's asleep?"*

Elroy told Christopher everything. He told about the ladder and the hedge and the sleeping oxen and the sleeping wagon driver and the sleeping butcher. Halfway through the story, Christopher started jumping up and down, he was so excited. When Elroy was finished, Christopher ran to his father. King Jasper CCX was talking to his last shepherd.

"*Sonora lives!*" Christopher yelled. "*She sleeps! She lives! She can tell us about the sheep! She can answer all my questions!*" He shouted to a squire, "*Saddle my horse!*"

But Christopher was too excited to wait. He ran after the squire and saddled his own horse. Then he rode to his father.

"Sire! I'm off to old Biddle Castle." He galloped away, calling behind him, "*To wake the sleeping princess!*"

Nine

After two days of hard riding, Christopher and his horse saw the hedge. The horse reared up and wouldn't go a step closer. Christopher jumped off and walked the rest of the way.

The hedge looked wicked. It was taller than the castle back home, and it was full of thick, hairy vines and thorns like spikes and waxy red berries that practically screamed, *"Poison!"*

Christopher wondered what the name of the vine was and what the berries were like. He smiled. Sonora would tell him.

It was going to take days to get inside. His sword wouldn't cut more than one vine before he'd have to sharpen it. Well, he might as well get started. He pulled the sword out of its sheath and walked toward the hedge, pointing the sword ahead of him.

It didn't touch so much as a leaf. A hole opened in the hedge and grew bigger and bigger until it was big enough for Christopher to step through.

Was it a trap? Was there really a princess named Sonora, or was a prince-eating ogress inside? Was Elroy the shepherd her messenger?

He had to go on. He had to find out—even if he died trying. He stepped through the hedge.

It snapped shut behind him. Oh no! It was as thick as before. He pointed his sword at it. Nothing happened. The hedge—or Sonora—wanted to keep him here.

He was at the edge of the moat. How was he supposed to get across? He could swim across if he was sure that the crocodiles were asleep, but he wasn't sure and he wasn't going to dive in to find out.

What? Lightning flashed out of the blue sky and struck a tree on the castle side of the moat. Whoa! The tree came down, making a rough bridge.

Christopher crossed slowly, stepping carefully between the branches. On the other side of the moat, he climbed a shoulder-high wall. Then he jumped down into a field of weeds so dense and tall that he didn't see Prince Melvin XX sleeping only a few feet away. The prince slept on the ground now. The bench he'd been lying on had rotted and fallen apart twenty years ago.

The weeds were brown and dying because it was November. Christopher wondered if this had once been the garden. He heard a rumbling. It stopped. There it was again. And again. Was it the breathing of the Sonora monster who lived in the castle?

He looked up. One of the castle's towers had crumbled, and an eagle perched atop another. Ivy climbed the walls. The pennants flying above the entrance archway were tattered rags.

Rumble. The earth trembled a little. *Rumble.*

Something rustled near Christopher's feet. Aaaa! A rat as big as a cat scampered across his boot. Christopher thought he should leave the garden. The bees were probably as big as pigeons.

Rumble.

The shepherd had said something about a wagon on the drawbridge and a butcher in the courtyard. He pushed through the weeds toward the entrance.

Rumble.

He reached the courtyard. There was the butcher! Possibly the Chief Royal Butcher, although you couldn't tell by the rags he was wearing. His shirt was so frayed and tattered that his belly showed through. He was slumped across his butcher block, next to a pile of bones. Fresh meat a hundred years ago, the prince thought.

And there was the carpenter, bent over a sawhorse, his saw at his feet. He was lucky he hadn't cut himself when he'd fallen asleep.

Rumble. Louder.

Or maybe the carpenter wasn't sleeping. Maybe they had all been turned to stone.

"Hey, wake up!" Christopher yelled. "Time to get up."

Nobody moved.

Rumble.

Christopher ran to the carpenter, who was closest. "Wake up!"

The man was filthy. His skin was coated with mud and dirt and dust and who-knew-what-else. Christopher wrapped a corner of his cloak around his hand. Then he pushed the carpenter's arm without letting his skin touch the carpenter's skin. The arm moved! It wasn't stone. He felt the carpenter's skin through the cloak. It was warm and soft—skin, not stone.

Christopher shook the arm. "Wake up! Listen! I command you, wake up!"

The carpenter slept on. He breathed in. His nostrils flared and his chest heaved. He breathed out, and the rumble started again.

It was the carpenter breathing! No, it couldn't be. One person couldn't breathe that loudly. Christopher backed up so he could watch the butcher and the carpenter at once.

The butcher breathed in and the carpenter breathed in. The butcher breathed out and the carpenter breathed out—at exactly the same time.

There were more people in the courtyard. Two men, possibly nobles, had been standing and talking when they'd fallen asleep. A cobbler had been shaping leather on a last. A laundress had been washing a mountain of clothes. Rags now.

They all breathed in and out at the same time. After a hundred years, they must have gotten into the habit of breathing together. That was what made the rumble.

Christopher went to each of them. He yelled in their ears. He shook them. He hollered, "Fire!" He yelled, "Food! Aren't you hungry?"

He yelled to the wagon driver and the oxen on the moat. But he was afraid to go to them. The drawbridge was rotting. If he stepped out on it, it might give way.

He tried to wake the dog, lying with his head on a bone. He tried to wake the cat. He told her about the huge rat that had run across his boot. The cat and the dog, Christopher decided, were sleeping because they were pets. The rats weren't pets, so they were awake.

Anyway, nothing worked. He couldn't wake anybody up.

What if Sonora wouldn't wake up either?

Ten

The castle doors were halfway off their hinges, so Christopher was able to open them only wide enough to slip through. Inside, he heard the flapping of wings. Bats. Birds too, from the droppings in the dust on the floor. He sneezed. He looked behind him, and there were his footsteps, sunk into a hundred years of dust. He took another step. His boots didn't make a sound because of the dust.

It was dim in here, in the great hall. The sunlight was weak through the grimy stained-glass windows. Even the broken windows didn't let in much light, because they were draped with cobwebs.

He crossed the hall. Where should he look first for Sonora, and how would he know her when he saw her?

People were everywhere, just as they would be on a busy day in Kulornia castle. "Wake up! Wake up!" he shouted. Nothing happened. He had stopped expecting anything, but he kept trying.

He shouted at everybody. But he shook only the women, and only women who looked like they might be a princess. He didn't bother with somebody who was making a bed or stirring an empty pot. He tried not to touch anybody with his hands. The people were all so filthy.

Nobody on the first floor would wake up, and it was probably useless to go upstairs and search the bedchambers. They had fallen asleep in the middle of the day, so why would anyone be in bed? But he had come all this way, and he had waited all his life to get his questions answered. Besides, he couldn't leave even if he wanted to, because of the hedge. He returned to the great hall and climbed the staircase.

Most of the bedchambers were empty. But Christopher found King Humphrey II and Queen Hermione II on the bed in the royal bedchamber. It was sweet, Christopher thought. They were holding hands. The king snored so loudly that he probably made half the rumbling. What was left of the curtains fluttered whenever he breathed out.

Finally Christopher came to Sonora's bedchamber. Finally he came to Sonora.

Generations of spiders had spun webs from post to post of her four-poster bed. Sonora slept under hundreds of layers of spiderwebs. The prince didn't know she was Sonora. All he knew was she was disgusting.

But she was probably noble, since she was on such a grand bed, or what used to be a grand bed. She might even be a princess. He had to do something. He coughed. Ahem.

Nothing happened.

He pulled out his sword and cut through the webs, which was a mistake. They all fell on top of her. Ugh. He brushed them away as well as he could with his cloak.

What was that on her stomach? Hmm, a wooden sign. He picked it up with his cloak and brushed it off. Dust and cobwebs and peeling paint came off. Drat! I should have been more careful, he thought.

He carried the sign to the window, where a broken pane let in a bit of sunlight. The paint had flaked off, but the wood was lighter where the paint had been. He could read it.

I am Princess Sonora. Kiss me, prince, and I shall be yours forever.

He didn't want her *forever*! And he certainly didn't want to *kiss* her.

Maybe he could live without getting his questions answered. He could train himself not to care so much. He'd hack his way through the hedge even if it took a month. They could find some other way to cure the sheep.

But what about all the people in the castle? And Princess Sonora, as sickening as she was? If he left, would they sleep till the end of time?

Let some other prince kiss her. Somebody who didn't mind getting ook and yuck and vech all over his face.

Who would that be?

Maybe he didn't have to kiss her. He touched her lips with the hilt of his sword. "Princess? Wake up. Your prince just kissed you."

Nothing happened.

He bent over her. He'd do it. But she wasn't going to be his forever.

What was that on her cheek and in the corner of her mouth? Spit? Bird droppings? Ugh!

He straightened up and turned to leave. He couldn't do it. He couldn't kiss her.

Eleven

"People float . . ."

Christopher whirled around. She was talking. She was awake!

Her eyes were closed. "People float because their essences . . ."

She was talking in her sleep. She had a sweet voice—a little hoarse, but sweet.

"People float because their essences are equal parts water and air. Stones sink . . ."

Even in her sleep she knew things! Sonora knows. And she was Sonora. And he was going to ask her everything.

He kissed her. He didn't think about it. He just did it. It wasn't so bad.

It was suddenly quiet. Oh, Christopher thought, they're all awake.

"Sleep is pleasant." Sonora's voice was thoughtful. "Hmm. The purpose of eyelids is to cover your eyes. If you didn't sleep, your eyelids would have little reason to close, except when the sun was too bright. But then you could just put your hands over your eyes. That's right. If you didn't have sleep, you wouldn't need eyelids, so you have to have sleep. I made a mistake before."

Christopher was thrilled. She was answering questions he'd never even thought of!

She raised her head. "It's hard to open my eyes. I knew this would happen. My eyelids are covered with cobwebs and worse, aren't they?" She sat up slowly. "Do you have any clean water?"

"No. I'm sorry."

She opened her eyes and smiled at him. "You're dirty too."

Her eyes were big and gray, and her teeth were white against her dirty skin. Her teeth looked clean. The inside of her mouth was probably clean too, so she wasn't dirty all over.

He looks nice, Sonora thought. There was something smiley about him. He was sort of handsome, but mostly he looked nice.

He bowed. "I'm Prince Christopher."

Through the broken window, they heard people calling to each other.

She stood and swept a graceful curtsy. "I am Sonora."

"The sheep of some of our shepherds are getting bald. Do you know why?"

"Baldness in sheep is caused by scissor ants."

She did know! "Really! What cures it?"

"String is their favorite food, not fleece. To get the scissor ants off the sheep, the shepherds have to put big balls of string near where the sheep graze. The ants will leave the sheep and go to the string. Then the shepherds can take the string and the ants away and get rid of them."

This was wonderful! "Do you like to answer questions?"

She smiled again. "I love to answer questions." Then she looked sad. "Only nobody likes to listen. They don't even like to ask."

"I love to ask, and I love to listen."

They smiled at each other.

"THE ANTS WILL LEAVE THE SHEEP AND
GO TO THE STRING."

The sign says she's mine forever, Christopher thought. I like that.

Sonora read the sign in Christopher's hand. That fairy Adrianna! The nerve of her! Sonora was about to say something nasty, but being so smart came to her rescue. She'd never exactly *belong* to anyone anyway, so it would be all right if the sign gave Christopher a good idea.

It did. He knelt on the dusty, cobwebby, bird-dropping-covered floor. "Will you marry me?"

Sonora started to say yes. Her loving heart loved this prince.

There were footsteps in the corridor.

She remembered. Prince Melvin XX!

The door opened. King Humphrey II and Queen Hermione II rushed in.

"Are you all right, dear?" the queen asked.

"You're dirty too," the king said. "Who's this?"

"He's Prince Christopher," Sonora said. "The sheep in his country are going bald from scissor ants."

Christopher stood up and bowed. "I am Christopher, crown prince of Greater Kulornia, and I've just asked the princess to marry me."

"But Melvin XX is crown prince of Kulornia," Queen Hermione II said.

Prince Melvin XX? Christopher thought. But he disappeared ages ago. Oh! He fell asleep too.

"Our daughter is betrothed to him. He—" King Humphrey II stopped in confusion. What did this fellow say about Greater Kulornia? Where did the "greater" come from?

Sonora said to Christopher, "Since one of the purposes of sheep is to make wool, you might wonder if a bald sheep is still a sheep."

Christopher nodded eagerly. "Is it?"

She nodded. "It is, because its other purpose is to become mutton stew, and it can still do that."

"That hadn't occurred to me." He couldn't stop smiling at her.

There were slow, heavy steps in the corridor.

Here he comes! Sonora thought. What can I do?

Prince Melvin XX came in, ducking to get through the doorway. "I fell asleep," he said slowly. "I'm dirty. My hose are torn. So is my doublet. So is my crown. So are—" He saw Christopher. "Who is he?"

Christopher bowed. "I am Christopher, crown prince of Greater Kulornia." Did Sonora want to marry this guy?

Prince Melvin XX drew his sword—*fast!* "I'm crown prince of Kulornia." But he still spoke slowly.

Sonora thought, Put that sword away! Don't hurt Prince Christopher!

Christopher thought, He probably won't kill me if I don't draw my sword. "And I just asked Princess Sonora to marry me."

Prince Melvin XX thought, I can't kill him if he doesn't draw his sword. I'm not a Bully. I'm a Man of Action. I used to be a Baby of . . .

Nobody said anything. Prince Melvin XX lowered his sword.

Sonora felt a little better. At least it wasn't pointing straight at Prince Christopher anymore. She thought, I can think of a way out of this. I'm not ten times as smart as anybody else for nothing.

Prince Melvin XX said, "I'm betrothed to Princess Sonora—"

Sonora had it! "Sir Melvin XX—"

"I'm Prince Melvin XX. Not Sir."

Sonora shook her head. "We slept for a hundred years, so you're not a prince anymore and I'm not a princess. You were betrothed to Princess Sonora, not to just plain Sonora. Right?"

"I don't know," said Prince or just plain Melvin XX.

She doesn't want to marry that great big tree trunk, Christopher thought. But does she want to marry me?

The king wondered if he was still a king, if Sonora wasn't a princess.

Sonora smiled at Melvin XX. "Your nature is to be strong and courageous."

Melvin XX nodded. "And Traditional and—"

She went on. "You will be a wonderful, traditional knight. You can have adventures and be brave and strong—"

"And Tall."

"And tall. I'm sure Prince Christopher would make you a knight."

Christopher didn't wait for Melvin XX to say yes or no. Usually Christopher did his dubbing with his sword. But he was afraid to draw it, because

Melvin XX still had his out. So Christopher reached way way up. With his naked, dirty hand he touched Melvin XX on his forehead.

"I, Prince Christopher, dub you Sir Melvin XX, knight of Greater Kulornia."

"Now you won't need me to write your proclamations," Sonora said.

Sir Melvin XX said, "I will be a good knight. A Brave knight. A Strong—"

Christopher knelt. "I've always been curious, but I've never wanted to know anything as much as this. Will you marry me, just plain Sonora?"

"Yes, I will." She nodded and took his hand. "In case you were wondering, sheep grow wool because of winter. The purpose of winter is to make ice, so people can have cherry or lemon ices in the summer. The purpose of wool is to keep sheep and then people warm while the ice is being made."

"Really? That makes so much sense."

She looks so happy, Queen Hermione II thought.

"Are we still a king?" King Humphrey II asked.

"Of course," Christopher said, standing up.

He'd work it out somehow.

Then it's all right, King Humphrey II thought. "In that case, we approve of the marriage. An excellent match."

Epilogue

As soon as King Humphrey II said he approved of the marriage, a gust of wind blew through the bedchamber, and the fairy Adrianna appeared. She beamed at everyone and crowed, "My gift was the best!" Then she married Sonora and Christopher on the spot.

After they both said "I do," and after they kissed, Christopher turned to Sonora. "Do you know if dragons burn the roofs of their mouths?"

"Yes, I know. No part of a dragon burns. You see, the essence of a dragon is fire . . ."

And they all lived happily ever after.

The End.